"He's My Son, Val, and a Boy Needs His Father."

"What you're saying is that you want to take him away from me."

"Not exactly. I want my son, but as you'd fight me every step of the way, I guess you'll have to come, too."

"And if I won't?"

"Just think it over, Val. And be prepared to move into my house by next weekend."

Her hand shot out, and she stared in horror at the livid marks on the tanned skin of his cheek. With a harsh exclamation, he pulled her against him, his lips descending toward hers.

"But first, I'll see to it that you get exactly what you deserve."

LINDA WISDOM

counts writing chief among her many interests. The world of the imagination has always been real to her, and with her novels this Southern California author is able to bring everyone's dreams of love and romance to life.

Dear Reader:

Silhouette Romances is an exciting new publishing venture. We will be presenting the very finest writers of contemporary romantic fiction as well as outstanding new talent in this field. It is our hope that our stories, our heroes and our heroines will give you, the reader, all you want from romantic fiction.

Also, *you* play an important part in our future plans for Silhouette Romances. We welcome any suggestions or comments on our books and I invite you to write to us at the address below.

So, enjoy this book and all the wonderful romances from Silhouette. They're for *you!*

Karen Solem
Editor-in-Chief
Silhouette Books
P. O. Box 769
New York, N.Y. 10019

LINDA WISDOM

Dancer in the Shadows

Silhouette Romance

Published by Silhouette Books New York

America's Publisher of Contemporary Romance

SILHOUETTE BOOKS, a Simon & Schuster Division of
GULF & WESTERN CORPORATION
1230 Avenue of the Americas, New York, N.Y. 10020

Distributed by Pocket Books

ISBN: 0-671-57049-8

10 9 8 7 6 5 4 3 2 1

America's Publisher of Contemporary Romance

Printed in the U.S.A.

Dancer in the Shadows

Chapter One

"Now *that* is a dress they won't forget at the party tonight." Shelly grinned at her friend. "You'll be able to hold your own with anyone there."

Valerie Hunter studied her reflection in the floor-length bedroom mirror. Dark brown hair was swept away from her face and pinned up in loose curls, emphasizing her dark-lashed green eyes. The Grecian-style gown of cream-colored silk clung to her slender curves, and only a minimum of makeup was necessary to accent her fresh beauty.

"It's the first party I've been to in years," she murmured, picking up a bottle of perfume.

"Mommy! Mommy!" A small boy ran into the room, skidding on his heels and looking up at Valerie with awe. "Oh, Mommy, you look so pretty," he whispered. "Sexy." His grin held pure adoration.

Her mouth curved into a smile at the sight of the little boy. "Sexy?" Her voice was teasing. "And where did you learn that word, Michael, my love?"

"At school," he replied artlessly. "Mary Davis says I'm sexy."

Shelly's short blonde curls danced as her head shook in amusement. She and Valerie exchanged knowing looks. "He's his father's son, Val," Shelly said quietly.

Valerie felt a pang as she thought of Sean. Why did thoughts of him invade her mind just when she felt she was getting over him? Yet, how could she forget him when all she had to do was look down at Michael? The small boy's hair was brown, with the same golden highlights, and his baby face showed signs of Sean's rugged features, although his eyes were the same green shade as hers.

Even after four years, she would still lie awake nights remembering the feel of Sean's possessive mouth on hers. His arms holding her against his lean, hard body as he whispered love words in his husky voice. His demand for an immediate response to his lovemaking—which she had gladly given. Her heart would still pound madly whenever she saw the back of a man's head with sun-kissed brown hair and the same broad build. She took a deep breath to banish the thoughts that could so easily drive her mad.

"What necklace are you going to wear?" Shelly's voice broke through her reflective thoughts.

"I'm not sure yet," she replied, rummaging through her jewelry chest. Her fingers stilled as they encountered a cold, hard stone. Trembling, she drew out a thin gold chain with a jade pendant hanging from it.

"Matches those cat's eyes of yours." Sean's voice spoke clearly in her mind as if he were standing next to her with his fingers caressing her bare shoulder.

Before she could lose her nerve, Valerie quickly clasped the pendant around her neck, the tear-shaped drop nestling in the discreet hollow between her breasts.

"That must be Craig for you," Shelly said, cocking her head at the sound of the doorbell. She quickly rose to her feet. "I'll get it."

Valerie picked up her evening bag and bent down to drop a kiss on the small boy's forehead. "You'll be good for Shelly tonight, won't you?" she smiled fondly at her son. "Don't forget to pick up all your toys before you go to bed."

She walked out to the living room, a smile of welcome on her face. "Hello, Craig."

His eyes roved slowly over her slim figure. "Very lovely," he murmured. "No one will be able to match you, Val."

Shelly grimaced behind Craig's back. Her dislike of Valerie's boss was no secret between the two friends. "Well, the two of you have a good time," she said brightly.

Craig's hand on Valerie's arm was possessive as he escorted her out of the apartment. "No wonder that boy is such a handful," he muttered, a dark look marring his blond good looks. "She isn't exactly the best influence, you know."

"Shelly loves Michael just as much as if he were her

own, Craig," Valerie said sharply. "He's nothing more than a normal boy. They're all active at this age."

"He needs a man around twenty-four hours a day," he persisted. "You know I'd be only too happy to handle a divorce for you if you would just give me the particulars—your husband's name, where he can be reached. You wouldn't even have to see him."

"I would prefer to handle it my way," she said tightly. "And if you continue in this vein, I would rather go back home than to the party."

One glance at her grim face told him she meant it, so he deftly changed the subject.

The country club was well known for its select membership, and the ornate plantation-style clubhouse always seemed to Val to embody this attitude. "I always feel as if I'm here on a pass," she said wryly as they walked up to the large double doors.

"You belong here just as much as any of them," Craig told her.

Inside, the men, handsome in their dinner jackets, and the women, resplendent in their expensive gowns and jewels, made a magnificent picture.

"A friend of mine from school is supposed to be here. I want you to meet him." Craig's eyes scanned the dance floor and the surrounding area. He slipped his arm around her waist in a possessive gesture. "Just as long as you remember who brought you, that is. Let's dance."

He led her out to the dance floor and took her in his arms. As they danced to the dreamy music, Valerie could feel a prickling sensation along the nape of her neck as if she were being observed. She glanced around, but saw nothing that could cause the feeling of unease.

"Hey, remember me?" Craig laughingly reminded her. "I'm that guy you're supposed to be madly in love with."

She laughed easily, causing the men around her to eye her with interest. After their dance, Craig got their drinks before they joined a group of his friends in lively conversation. Then Craig straightened as he spied someone across the room.

"Come on, darling. I see him now."

Valerie allowed herself to be led by one hand, keeping her wineglass in the other. The warm smile on her face froze as she saw the man Craig was approaching. Tall and disturbing in a white dinner jacket, the man stood near the open French windows. The bright lights shone on his brown hair, highlighting the sun-bleached strands that lay carelessly above his darkly tanned forehead. The expression on his face was openly cynical, the dark brown eyes almost black in their coldness. A voluptuous black-haired woman in her early thirties, dressed in a red strapless gown of clinging silk, hung onto his arm, seeming very much a part of him.

Valerie gripped her wineglass tightly, trembling as his eyes rested on her pinned-up hair with amusement. Automatically, she lifted her hand to her hair in a defensive gesture.

"Sean, glad to see you again," Craig greeted the man, bringing a reluctant and pale Valerie forward. "Val, this is Sean Hunter; Sean, Valerie Hunter, my secretary. Seems you two share the same name, but that better be all you share. Valerie's a very important part of my life."

"Craig!" She blushed hotly at his words.

"Miss Hunter." The cold voice sent shivers along her spine.

"Mrs. Hunter," she corrected stiffly.

"Running around with married women now, are you, Craig?" Sean drawled lazily as he cocked an eyebrow at the other man.

"Not exactly," he laughed.

"As it seems we've been forgotten, I'm Felicia Everst." The dark-haired woman smiled coolly at Valerie, and Valerie noticed the wide gold band on the other woman's hand.

"Mrs. Hunter, would you care to dance?"

Valerie's head snapped upward at the icy tones. "I don't know," she said faintly, knowing that the last thing she wanted was to have him touch her.

Ignoring her protest, he clasped her wrist with a steel hand, leading her to the dance floor. Valerie groaned inwardly as the band began to play a softly sensuous love song. She shrank away from him as she felt his muscular thighs burn through the thin material of her dress. Her nose detected the faint aroma of a woodsy cologne mixed with cigarettes and his clean male smell, bringing back so many painful memories.

"You've done quite well for yourself, Mrs. Hunter." Sean's icy voice flayed her already bruised nerves. His fingers dug cruelly into her waist, but she didn't show her pain by so much as a flickering eyelid.

Valerie kept her eyes on the front of his ruffled shirt,

her body moving sinuously with his as they had done years before. When the music stopped, he checked her retreat by gripping her wrist tightly. "Thank you for the dance, Mrs. Hunter," he said coldly, his features devoid of expression. "I'm sure we'll meet again." The tone held a threat, causing her to back away in fright as he released her arm.

Holding back the violent tears that threatened to fall, Valerie fled through the open doors, not stopping until she reached a far dark corner of the garden. Breathing deeply, she stared unseeingly ahead in order to calm her frazzled nerves. A few moments later, she turned as she heard footsteps behind her. Before she could speak, a pair of hands grabbed her arms in a rough grip as her mouth was imprisoned by a pair of lips ruthlessly parting hers. She struggled in the embrace, tears streaming down her face as her mouth was bruised by punishing kisses.

She was suddenly released and the figure disappeared silently into the darkness. Fighting the rising nausea, Valerie stumbled to a side door near the powder room. Relieved to find it empty, she dropped to a pink velvet stool before the large lighted mirror, letting the tears flow unchecked. When she felt calmer, she repaired her eye makeup and lipstick before venturing outside. She held her breath as she looked around for Sean and felt relieved not to see him anywhere.

"There you are." Craig approached her, a warm smile on his face. "I've been looking for you."

"I—uh—I wanted to repair my makeup," she replied weakly.

"Do you feel all right? You look pale." He appeared concerned.

"No, I'm fine."

Valerie managed to get through the evening with an artificial smile on her strained face, and she drank more wine than was good for her. She was grateful when Craig suggested leaving.

"I told you the party would be fun," he told her, not noticing her strained features. "I'm glad you were able to meet Sean. He's a great person."

No, he isn't a great person! Valerie's nerves screamed out. He's cruel and unfeeling!

When they reached the apartment house, she pleaded a headache, slipping out of the car and leaving behind a disappointed Craig.

"I'll see you Monday, Craig." She smiled, desiring only the solitude of her room.

Once inside the apartment, Valerie's face reflected the pain she felt. Moving quietly, she stopped first in the small room where her son slept. She carefully arranged the covers over his shoulders before tiptoeing out.

Valerie was grateful that Shelly was already asleep so she wouldn't have to endure any questions about the party. Once inside the bedroom they shared, she slipped off her dress, letting it fall to the floor in a careless heap. Reaching behind her neck, she was dismayed to find her jade pendant missing. She looked around the floor and, not seeing it, decided that the slender chain must have snapped during the struggle. She felt tears pricking at the back of her eyes.

She quickly pulled the pins out of her hair before she

crawled into bed. Curled into a tight ball, she fought the mounting tears as her mind wandered back to that time four years before . . . that time when Sean Hunter entered her life.

At twenty, all Valerie's thoughts were for her upcoming audition at the ballet school. She had no time to look around beautiful San Francisco. When she wasn't practicing at the school, she was relaxing on the beach with her friend Shelly and the four other girls they shared a house with.

She had her life all planned out for her—until the night of the barbecue on the beach. Enjoying a late-night swim, one of the boys, Ron, had too much to drink and became friendlier than Valerie wanted. Then a tall, dark figure had interrupted Ron's attentions, sending him away and then walking Val back to her friends.

How could she forget that first time she had seen him? The firelight illuminated a bronzed face, and a slightly crooked nose, as if it had been broken at some time. The angular cheekbones led to a frankly sensual mouth with a hint of cruelty. His firm jaw completed a no-nonsense face. Not handsome, but arresting. A man no woman could ever forget—or want to. His tall, lean build was emphasized by a dark shirt covering a powerful chest. His dark slacks molded to his muscular thighs and lean hips. With one thumb hooked through a belt loop, he had the appearance of a lithe jungle animal. She judged him to be in his early thirties and over six feet tall. She could still remember how the expression in his dark eyes had caused her legs to tremble. Even with her innocence, Valerie knew he would be a man to change her life—even though she didn't know his name.

Valerie's thoughts were of the mysterious man the day she auditioned for the academy. Her parents had been killed in an automobile accident six months before and would not know that their dreams for their only daughter were at last being realized. When her name was called, she licked suddenly dry lips and approached the center of the rehearsal hall.

The toes of one foot rested against the heel of the other in the classic fifth position. The soft strains of a valse from *The Sleeping Beauty* drifted through the air. Unconsciously, a face came to her mind and she was dancing for *him.* Her turns were as graceful as if she danced on air. Her hair gleamed in the light. Her face was flushed, as if he were watching her now. What was he, then? A ruthless duke sitting in a large, carved wooden chair watching one of his chattels dance for him?

Haunted by a man she had seen only once, Valerie was still in a daze when she left the academy. Outside, she was momentarily blinded by the bright sunlight and rummaged in her purse for her sunglasses. Walking down the stone steps, she didn't see the tall, imposing figure on the sidewalk.

"Taxi, lady?" A lazy drawl brought her head up to face a pair of dark brown eyes. He was leaning back against the hood of an expensive, low-slung sports car, his long legs crossed in front of him.

"How—how did you know I was here?" A feeling of giddy excitement rose inside her at the sight of her rescuer.

"I saw you go in earlier and I was curious to see what made a little girl run so fast," he replied smoothly, taking the tote bag out of her nerveless fingers. "Right now, you don't look as if you've had any food today."

"I overslept this morning," Valerie said breathlessly. Had he stayed here for the past three hours just to see her? Yet, he didn't seem to be the type of man to wait for any woman.

"Then you have no excuse for turning down my lunch invitation." He opened the car door, assisting her into the passenger's seat.

"I—but I don't know you," she protested weakly, her skin tingling from his brief touch. "I don't even know your name."

After he slid behind the steering wheel, he half-turned in the seat, dark eyes with gold flecks turned to her flushed face. "Sean Hunter, at your service, ma'am." He inclined his head formally. "Now, as to you, my water sprite, what may I call you?"

"Valerie Rhodes," she whispered, still under his spell.

"Well, Valerie Rhodes, I hope you like seafood."

The afternoon was a magical one for Valerie. Over a seafood lunch at a famous restaurant at Fisherman's Wharf, she learned that Sean Hunter was an army engineer stationed at the Presidio and evidently traveled a great deal. Her twenty years were nothing compared to his thirty-two as they discussed her hopes to be admitted to the ballet school and her plans for the future. After a delicious lunch, they walked around the wharf and visited the familiar sights of the waterfront area.

"What would you say to Ghirardelli Square?" Sean

asked suddenly. He noted her hesitancy. "Or do you have someone waiting for you?" His tone meant someone male. She was unaware of the change in his manner as he watched conflicting expressions cross her face.

"No, I just thought there must be someone else you'd rather be with than me." Her low voice indicated her confusion. Why would he want to spend the day with her? She certainly couldn't be the type of girl he was used to spending his time with.

He suddenly gripped her chin, forcing her eyes up to meet his own dark ones. "Cat eyes, if I didn't want to be with you, I wouldn't be here," Sean murmured, his warm breath caressing her face.

Valerie held her breath, thinking he was going to kiss her. She felt disappointed when he removed his hand, saying abruptly, "I suggest we get back to the car and head for Ghirardelli Square."

Near the large, popular tourist attraction, known for the making of chocolate candy and now a center full of shops of every description, Sean pulled into an underground parking lot where they left the car.

Valerie's eyes grew huge looking around at the various articles displayed in store windows. In one jewelry shop, she lingered over a jade teardrop pendant edged in delicate gold filigree. The amount written on the small white tag told her, though, that it was far beyond her means.

When the late afternoon sun set behind the mountains, the evening's cool air suggested it was time for dinner. Sean steered her toward a nearby Italian restaurant with a warm and homey atmosphere.

Valerie relaxed during the large meal of minestrone soup and veal parmigiana accompanied by a bottle of red wine. When they left the restaurant to return to the car, her face was becomingly flushed from the wine.

The parking lot was cool and she shivered slightly while waiting for Sean to unlock the car. Noticing her action, he reached inside, grabbed a dark brown suede jacket, and settled it around her shoulders. His hands stayed momentarily on her shoulders before sliding slowly down her arms to go around her waist under the jacket. Keeping his eyes on her upturned face, ethereal in the dim light, he gently pulled her unresisting form toward him. He leaned back against the car, keeping his arms around her. Valerie stared mesmerized at his descending mouth as it settled warmly and lightly on her lips. The touch was softly sensual, wreaking havoc with her senses. Feeling her response, he expertly parted her lips, exploring the sweetness within. Her arms crept up over his chest to his shoulders, winding around his neck, her fingers raking through his crisp hair. His woodsy aftershave mixed with his male scent to assault her senses, causing her body to tremble. Sean's lips trailed along her jawline to the sensitive cord in her neck, nibbling gently. Valerie's hand crept down, unconsciously unbuttoning several buttons of his shirt, letting her fingers seek the warmth of his body. Sean's expert caresses were awakening new emotions inside her. Suddenly he pressed the side of her face against his chest. She could hear the erratic heartbeat under her ear, matching her own racing pulse. Sean's hands lifted, deftly pulling the pins out of her hair, letting it tumble free past her shoulders. His fingers raked the silky tresses before cupping her nape, raising her face to his. A lean, brown forefinger traced her lips, swollen from his passionate kisses.

"Val," Sean said thickly against her hair, "you seem so special that I don't want to let you go. Come home with me."

Still bemused from his lovemaking, she didn't realize the true meaning of his words. "It's terribly late and I should be getting back to the house," she replied huskily, rubbing her cheek against his hair-roughened chest where the buttons were still undone.

"If you feel the same way later, I'll take you home then," he chuckled. "Or we'll just wait until after breakfast."

As the bald truth of his statement hit her, Valerie pulled away abruptly, trying to hide her burning face. She felt burning shame at her abandoned response. Sean's face creased in puzzlement at her stiff withdrawal, his eyes narrowed in speculation.

"Val, are you a virgin?" he asked bluntly, bending his head slightly to study her face.

"That's a pretty stupid question to ask a girl in this day and age." She laughed shakily, still refusing to look at him. A taste of bitterness was in her mouth. "I admit I may not be considered experienced enough for someone as sophisticated as yourself, but if you don't mind being patient with someone who's still in the learning stage . . ."

"Shut up!" Sean's hands gripped her shoulders roughly, shaking her none too gently, until tears rolled down her cheeks. She choked back a sob at the look of black fury on his face. "Don't you realize that if we had kept on, it would have been easy for me to make love to you whether you wanted me to or not? I'm not a saint, and I've slept with my share of women. But it didn't mean that I loved them, only that I made love *to* them," he stated crudely. "I am very much a hypocrite about the woman I will marry. I don't want to wonder how many men she's been with before me. I want to be the one to initiate her into the passions of lovemaking. You have a very precious gift. Don't abuse it or throw it away. Save it for that special man one day."

Sean's bruising grip loosened as he noticed the damp streaks on her cheeks and her trembling lips. Uttering an oath under his breath, he brushed his fingertips lightly across her face and brought the salty wetness to his lips. He groaned softly, wrapping his arms around her body, bringing her back against his chest.

"Sean?" Her low voice questioned his sudden tenderness.

"Ssh!" His hand stroked her hair lightly. A low chuckle rumbled deeply in his chest. "I haven't kissed a girl in a parking lot since high school. You make me feel old, infant."

"You're not old," Valerie protested drowsily, content with his arms around her.

"I think I'd better take you home while I still have some common sense left," he said ruefully, putting her reluctantly from him.

As Sean drove out of the parking lot and headed for the main road, Valerie sat back in the seat, still feeling the spell he had wrapped around her, as warm as the coat. She closed her eyes, happy to have her hand warmly enclosed in his.

"Val"—a low voice drifted through her sleep-drugged mind—"you're home."

Her face turned in the direction of the voice as light kisses were rained over her face, teasing the corner of her mouth before settling fully on her slightly parted lips.

"Come to Sutro Park with me tomorrow," he murmured against her mouth, his breath mingling with hers.

"Can you bear to spend the day with a mere infant?" she teased.

Sean's reply was a drugging kiss, forcing her to respond. He was trembling when he finally released her. "What mere infant?" he muttered hoarsely, nuzzling her throat. "You're a witch. A witch capable of casting crazy spells over me."

Sean released her, then got out of the car and walked around the front to open her door. His dark, craggy features appeared unearthly in the ghostly moonlight. But she felt no fear of him.

When Valerie reached the front door, Sean's hand encircled her wrist, drawing her back toward him. "I'll pick you up at nine," he murmured, his fingers caressing the soft inner skin. "Right now, I suggest you go inside before I change my mind and carry you off to my place, where I doubt we would talk very much." His kiss brushed lightly across her lips with a promise of more to come. She slipped off his jacket and handed it to him. He grinned, his teeth flashing white in his bronzed face as he gently pushed her inside. "Tomorrow," he said softly.

She stood in the doorway, watching him move with lithe grace to his car. Soon the powerful engine sprang to life and roared down the road. She watched the red tail lights disappear and touched her fingertips to her swollen lips. She slowly closed the door, a dreamy expression on her face.

Sean became a part of Valerie's life. When he was free from his duties at the base, he would show her parts of the famous city that she hadn't known existed. Her breath caught in her throat when they would walk along and Sean would lift her hand, pressing his lips against her open palm, sending liquid fire through her veins. She soon didn't want to think of what the future would be like without him.

One of their favorite haunts became the zoo. Watching the panthers pace restlessly, she glanced sideways under her lashes, comparing the tall, lean man standing next to her to the graceful jungle animals. A dark shirt and pants emphasized his wide shoulders and lean hips. His forearms were resting on the top of the fence, the fingers linked together. Sean's dark brown hair reflected gold highlights in the bright sunlight. Valerie's eyes traveled over his strong face, noting dark eyebrows over expressive eyes, the faint bump on his nose, and the cynical twist to his sensual mouth.

"Keep it up and I won't be responsible for the consequences." A low voice invaded her thoughts.

"What do you mean?" She looked up coyly.

"You know perfectly well what I mean, so don't play the fool with me." His words were clipped, cold.

Hurt by his sudden anger, she lowered her head to hide the tears pricking her eyelids. The back of a brown hand gently stroked her cheek.

"People will think I beat you, cat eyes," he murmured. "Strange, you seem so self-assured, yet you're such a little girl underneath. I have trouble finding out which you really are."

"Sometimes I'm not even sure myself," she whispered, her eyes still downcast.

"Let's go," Sean said crisply.

As the day passed, Valerie could feel his continued withdrawal, hurting her even more. In self-defense, she also withdrew, not caring that she was behaving like the child he was determined to consider her.

"How about some dinner?" Sean's brusque voice interrupted her feelings of self-misery.

"I don't care." Valerie shrugged her shoulders indifferently.

Sighing heavily, he directed her to a popular Chinese restaurant. Their meal was silent as she idly picked at her food. Sean pushed his plate aside, lighting a cigarette, and leaned back in his chair, his eyes narrowed against the smoke curling upward.

"I think you've played with your food long enough," he said abruptly, signaling the waiter. "Let's get out of here."

"I'm not finished," Valerie mumbled.

"Yes, you are," he said flatly.

Outside in the cool air, he looked down at her set features as if regretting his harsh words. "Would you care to look through some of the shops?"

"I want to go home," she replied tightly, walking away from him.

When they arrived at the car, she stared numbly ahead as he unlocked the passenger's door. She could feel his eyes on her, but refused to look up. Muttering a savage oath under his breath, he pulled her roughly into his arms, his hard mouth bruising her soft one. Struggling against the steel bands holding her, Valerie could feel the tears roll down her face in mute protest at his burning kiss. A soft moan was torn from her throat as he lifted his lips a fraction above hers.

"You're a witch, Valerie Rhodes, and by all rights I should be miles away from you," he muttered thickly, burying his face in her softly scented hair.

"Then why aren't you?" she asked breathlessly, resting her cheek against his chest.

"Because I *am* a fool." He quickly released her and pushed her into the car.

The silence was heavy during the drive back to Valerie's house. Sean shut off the engine, staring straight ahead.

"Will I see you tomorrow?" she asked softly.

"I don't think so, Val." His voice was bleak.

"The—the next day, then?" She feared his answer.

"No, Val."

The final ring to his words struck her heart with a chill.

"A-are you going away?" Valerie could barely whisper because of the lump in her throat.

"It isn't wise for us to see each other anymore." Sean's voice was painfully gentle. "You need to be with younger men. A girl as beautiful as you shouldn't have any problem finding someone."

Valerie bit her lower lip to still its trembling.

"You're a sweet kid. I don't want to hurt you," he said heavily, turning to place his fingertips against her cheek.

Childishly, she slapped his hand away, her eyes bright with unshed tears. "I suppose I should be grateful that you've been so kind to a child like me," Valerie said bitterly. "And now your good deed is done. I'm sure you'll understand why I can't be polite right now like the good little girl I am and thank you for a nice time."

"Val!" She ignored him as she flung herself out of the car and ran for the front door, thankful to find it unlocked. Once inside, she flipped the latch and leaned against the door, breathing heavily. It seemed ages before the car's powerful engine sprang to life, revving up more than necessary before roaring away.

When she finally slipped into bed that night, the tears still refused to fall.

As the days passed, Valerie's misery became more evident. Even Shelly, her closest friend, couldn't bring her back to life. "Considering the short time you knew him, you fell awfully hard," she ventured one day.

"At least I didn't break any bones," Valerie said wryly. "With luck, the scars won't even show."

"A group of us are going up to the Napa Valley tomorrow. Come with us," Shelly urged.

"No, thanks." She smiled faintly, shaking her head. "I'll be fine, Shel. Honest."

Chapter Two

The next day, Valerie found the silence of the house unbearable. She finally escaped outside to walk along the beach.

After walking a short distance, she dropped down to build a sand castle. During her task, she had the uneasy feeling of being watched, but quick glances around the beach and at a large house sitting on the cliff proved fruitless. Turning back to her lopsided castle, she squashed it down with her hands before looking up to stare out over the water.

"Val?" The deep voice from behind caused her to stiffen.

"Go away," she managed to choke out, keeping her eyes straight ahead.

"Val, talk to me." His voice was more insistent than coaxing.

"You didn't want to see me anymore," she said stubbornly, refusing to look up at him.

Sean walked around her and squatted on his heels to face her. Still refusing to look at him, she concentrated on a point over his left shoulder.

"You can't look out there all day, infant." His voice was caressing.

She tipped her head slightly to let a curtain of hair fall, hiding her face from his eyes. "It's a public beach," she muttered. "Just go away."

A lean brown hand shot out, jerking her head around to face him fully. Green eyes full of confusion and hurt faced brown eyes, seeing gold glints dance in anger.

"You're acting like a spoiled brat who needs a good spanking," Sean said tightly. "And, as you said, it's a public beach."

"You didn't want to see me anymore," she whispered. "And I *don't* want to see you. So you can just go back to where you came from."

"Do you mean that?" His face appeared carved from stone.

"Yes." Valerie choked out the word.

Sean studied her set face for several moments before suddenly releasing her chin. He slowly rose to his feet and walked up the beach without a backward glance. Valerie turned wide-eyed, fighting the tears threatening to overflow. Sean, clad only in a pair of jeans cut off above the knees, walked sure-footedly in the soft sand toward a wooden stairway winding upward to the house sitting on the cliff.

"No, please don't go, Sean," she cried under her breath, then raised her voice. "Sean!"

He slowly turned around, but the stony look on his rugged features told her that she would have to make the first move. Valerie chewed her lower lip, fighting an inner battle with her pride. She rose slowly, tears streaming down her face.

"You told me to leave you alone," he said harshly, his hands on his hips.

"Only because you said it would be better if I saw other men. You practically called me a child." Her pride lost out to her emotions as she walked slowly toward him. Curiosity soon got the best of her. "Why are you here?"

"You didn't seem to want to know a few moments ago," Sean said roughly.

Valerie childishly wiped her damp face with the back of her hand as she stopped in front of his rigid figure.

"Do you want me to go away?" he demanded.

"No." Her voice trembled.

His eyes softened as his fingertips touched the salty dampness below her eyes. His hand curled around the nape of her neck, drawing her closer to him. Valerie stiffened at his touch.

"Don't fight me, Val," Sean said huskily, touching her trembling lips with his firm, warm ones with fleeting pressure.

"But you said—" She choked, still unable to stop her tears.

"The devil with what I said." He pulled her hard against him, stilling her tearful protests with his mouth, rough against hers.

Valerie's mind whirled as Sean's mouth moved sensually over hers, demanding a response she freely gave. Wrapping her arms around his neck, she arched her body against his, wanting to be as close to him as possible. She moaned softly in protest when he lifted his head a fraction. Although her senses were still swimming from his masterful kiss, a small part of her mind was still puzzled by his sudden appearance.

"Why did you come here?" she asked breathlessly.

"We need to talk," he said firmly, pulling her back against him.

"Is that what we did the last time?" Bitterness tinged her voice.

"Come on," Sean said impatiently, pulling her up the stairs.

Valerie's eyes lifted upward. "You live up there?" Her voice ended in a surprised squeak.

"I have the loan of it," he said briefly, tugging on her hand. "Are you coming?"

The tremulous smile on her face was her answer as she followed him up the stairs.

Once inside the large, sunlit living room, Valerie looked around with interest at the clever blending of earth tones brightened by touches of orange.

"I'll put some steaks on the barbecue if you want to throw together a salad or whatever," Sean suggested, steering her toward the kitchen. "You can cook, can't you?"

"Of course I can!" she said indignantly before she realized he was teasing.

Valerie enjoyed rummaging through the compact kitchen as she found the makings for a tossed green salad and garlic bread. She started as arms encircled her waist, pulling her back against a hard, bare chest.

"I think I'd rather eat you for dinner," Sean muttered against her neck. "I want to lock you away and keep you all to myself." He turned her around in his arms and pressed a lingering kiss on her lips. "However, I'd better get back to the steaks." He was reluctant to release her.

Valerie watched him leave with a confused look in her eyes. She picked up plates and silverware to set the table as the phone rang.

"Val, would you answer that, please?" Sean called over his shoulder. "If I leave these steaks now, they'll burn for sure."

She hurried over to a dark brown telephone sitting on a table near the couch. "Hunter residence," she said crisply.

"Jay? Hi, it's Anne. I heard that Sean's back in town." A very feminine, husky voice purred in her ear. "When did the darling arrive?"

"This isn't Jay," Valerie said stiffly, a cold knot developing in her stomach. "Would you like to speak to Sean?"

"Oh, he's there?" The voice sounded surprised at first, then turned to light amusement. "Yes, actually, I would."

Valerie set the receiver down and walked woodenly out to the terrace. "Someone named Anne would like to speak to you." She tried to make her voice sound casual.

"Tell her I can't—" Sean looked up, spying her set facial expression. "Okay, I'll talk to her." He hurriedly piled the cooked meat on a platter, pushing it into her hands. "Want to put this on the table for me?" He walked over to the phone and picked up the receiver.

"Hi, Anne." Was it her imagination, or did his voice sound irritated? "Oh, about six weeks ago. . . . No, she's still in Spain. . . . Friday night? I don't think so." Sean bent down, picking up a cigarette pack and extracting one before picking up a table lighter. He exhaled the smoke slowly through his nostrils. "No, really I don't—" He sighed heavily. "Well, I'll let you know. Good-bye, Anne."

While he had been on the phone, Valerie had seated herself at the table, her face a mask of indifference. Sean left the room for a moment and returned wearing a dark gold knit shirt that accented the breadth of his shoulders. Casting a lazy grin at her, he picked up his plate and silverware, which had been set across from her, and placed them on her right. "Too far away. And I forgot something."

Valerie listened to him whistling in the kitchen and bit her lower lip to keep the tears back. She was aware that Sean was sexually attractive to women, and that he was man enough to accept whatever they offered him. But he was the first man to stir her emotionally and physically, and her heart didn't want to accept what her mind told her.

Sean returned to the table, carrying a bottle of red wine and two glasses. "I promise not to ask for your identification." He filled her glass partway.

If Sean noticed Valerie's stiff silence during the meal, he gave no indication. He applied himself to his steak and praised her culinary talents. She discovered that frequent sips of wine helped alleviate the pain she felt inside, especially when she poured herself a second glass.

"Is Jay your girl friend?" she asked artlessly.

"Does it matter?" he asked huskily, a strange light in his eyes.

"Of course not. I was just curious." Valerie concentrated on her steak. "After all, it's no concern of mine if she lives here," she added recklessly, reaching for her wineglass only to find it empty. "May I have more wine, please?"

"I think you've had enough," Sean said lazily, moving the bottle out of her reach.

"I'm not a child," she said haughtily.

"In many ways you still are." His eyes swept over her flushed features.

Sean hadn't said that Jay was his girl friend, or that she lived here. Yet, from what she had seen of the house, there appeared to be more feminine touches than masculine. Valerie stood up quickly, gathering up the now-empty dishes. "I'll just wash these," she murmured.

"I'll help you." He rose to his feet.

"No, there aren't very many," Valerie protested, anxious to have something to do.

In the kitchen, she lingered over the task as long as she could. When she finally returned to the living room, Sean was seated on the couch, his long legs stretched out in front of him. "Come here." His expression was frankly sensual as he patted the cushion next to him.

She sat down, keeping plenty of distance between them. Sean arched a surprised eyebrow, but said nothing.

"I—uh—I probably should be getting back," she stammered nervously.

"Why?" Sean's eyes narrowed. "Why the sudden change, Val?"

"Please, Sean, I can't stay here," she pleaded. "I understand now why you didn't want to see me anymore. After all, if the girl who lives with you found out, there could be problems."

His puzzled features relaxed in comprehension. With one swift movement, he pulled Valerie onto his lap. "I think you and my sister would get along very well. You both enjoy jumping to the wrong conclusion," he murmured.

"Sister?"

"Janine, Jay for short. This is her house," he explained.

"You have a sister?" Valerie said faintly.

"That's what my parents told me when they brought her home from the hospital," he replied drily. "Feel better now?"

"It really didn't matter." She affected an indifferent shrug.

"Liar," Sean said huskily. "And I can prove it."

Her head reeled as his mouth descended on hers. He parted her lips with ease, exploring the softness slowly, as if savoring a dessert or a fine wine.

"All I dream about is a girl with hair dark and sleek as a seal's coat, and big green cat eyes," he said hoarsely. "A mouth that invites kissing and a body made to be loved. I'm thirty-two years old and should know better, but I'm caught in your witch's spell."

He bent her backward until his weight became a

warm blanket on her pliant body, his hands molding her to his hard male outline. Her skin burned where his hands caressed her bare back under her T-shirt. Valerie had never imagined that a kiss could drown her in such deep, sensual feelings. She twined her arms around his neck, letting her fingers rake through his crisp, dark hair. His kiss deepened, sending her senses whirling. Suddenly, he lifted his head and moved away.

"Sean?" She felt hurt by his abrupt rejection.

"One of us is going to have to show some control, Val," he smiled wryly. "And I guess it'd better be me, no matter how it hurts. I think I'd better walk you home."

He rose to his feet, then pulled her upward. As her body swayed invitingly toward him, his hands rested on her shoulders.

"No, Val," Sean said firmly. "We'd better leave now while I still have some scruples."

A smile of contentment was on Valerie's face as they walked along the beach, Sean's arm thrown possessively around her waist.

"I've been invited to a party Friday night," he informed her. "Go with me."

"Is that a request or an order?" she teased.

A smile touched the corners of his mouth. "I'll pick you up at eight. I'm going to be busy at the base until then," he explained, "so I doubt I'll see you before Friday."

They stopped in front of her door. "Then I should have something to remember you by," Valerie said huskily, lifting her face.

"Witch," Sean groaned, crushing her against him.

* * *

Valerie could feel butterflies gathering in her stomach that Friday as she gazed up at the large, pretentious house that spoke of great wealth, a wealth accumulated over the years.

"Sean, I—" She caught his arm, unable to voice her fears.

A fleeting smile passed over the rugged features, softening them momentarily as he grasped her hand and squeezed it. "Later," Sean murmured, the one word a promise.

As they entered the house, Valerie was grateful for her choice of dress. The floor-length, A-line skirt was deep mauve velvet with a top of pale rose with a lacy camisole of a deeper color worn underneath. A soft leather belt of deep mauve emphasized her slender waist. The deep V neckline ended just above the shadowy cleft between her breasts.

A butler greeted them at the door, directing them to a large room to one side. Sean's hand at Valerie's elbow tightened possessively as several men gave her open looks of interest. He glanced down, seeing a slit in the front of her skirt opening to reveal a goodly portion of slender leg as she walked beside him.

"Lady, you're going to need a bodyguard," he said wryly, bringing a smile to her face. "And I'm not exactly the best man for the job."

A woman in her late twenties approached them, ethereal in ice-blue. Her silver-blonde hair was fashioned in a smooth chignon, revealing cold, patrician features. Her heavily made-up eyes paused to consider Valerie piece by piece. They dismissed her as unimportant before settling warmly on Sean.

"Darling, you came after all," she said throatily, her hand fluttering on his arm. "And I see you brought a—friend."

"Anne Carson, Valerie Hunter." Sean smoothly evaded her grasp by turning to Valerie. "Anne is a friend of Janine's and is our hostess."

"I'm happy to meet you, Miss Carson," Valerie said politely.

"Such a sweet child." Anne ignored her. "Are you sure her parents will allow her to be out so late?"

Valerie's temper began rising as she watched Anne press herself intimately against Sean. "If you'll excuse us, I'd like to dance with Val." He smiled coolly at Anne.

Sean kept his arm around her waist as he steered her outside where the dancing was being held. He drew her into his arms, keeping her head against his chest as they moved together to the slow melody. Sean's breath was warm against her cheek.

When the music stopped, he led her over to several couples he knew who seemed genuinely friendly. Valerie saw a new side of Sean as she listened to him discuss his travels to Greece, France, Spain, and his latest assignment in Panama. She felt inferior to the worldly man standing close to her, his arm possessively around her waist.

Later that evening, Valerie excused herself to go to the powder room to freshen her lipstick. She had just patted a stray curl into place when Anne swept into the black and silver room, gracefully seating herself on a black velvet bench.

"You're much too innocent to keep Sean for long,"

she stated bluntly. "He's an excellent lover, and I don't intend to lose him to some little schoolgirl."

"Perhaps he wants a change for the better." Val's voice sounded calmer than she would have believed possible as she snapped her evening bag shut. She rose from the dressing table, walking to the door, wanting to get as far as possible from Anne.

"You don't have what it takes to hold a man like Sean," Anne told her shrilly.

"Then I'll have to let him teach me, won't I?" she said quietly, leaving the room.

Across the crowded room, Sean noticed Valerie's tense face and was beside her instantly, his hand on her arm. "Would you like to go?" he murmured, his concerned eyes on her face.

Anne walked out of the powder room and Sean glanced quickly from Anne's livid face to Val's strained one before, putting two and two together, he asked, "What did she say to you?" His face darkened and for a moment Val was afraid that he might actually say something to Anne.

"Nothing, Sean. Really. Please, let's just go." Her voice was pleading.

His black temper was barely under control as he almost pushed her into the car. Once inside, his hands gripped the steering wheel until the knuckles whitened. Valerie was frightened by the look of cold rage on his face.

"Sean?" She reached out tentatively, gently stroking his cheek with her fingertips. She could see the tension gradually leave his body as he rested the back of his head against the seat.

"I'm sorry, Val." He captured her hand, bringing the palm to his lips. "I didn't realize she could be so vindictive or that she would take it out on you."

"She said you were lovers," Val said in a low voice, feeling an ache at the back of her throat.

"We were." His flat reply brought her fresh pain. "But it was over long ago when I saw what a cold-hearted creature she really is." He turned back, switching on the engine and putting the car in gear. He drove until he reached a small park on a hill and parked the car nearby.

"Val, look at me." As her eyes swept upward, he turned in the seat and drew her across his lap. His fingers tangled in her hair so that she couldn't escape the insistent kiss that branded her as his. He expertly parted her lips, his breath mingling with hers. Valerie's arms crept around his neck; her fingers curled in his hair as she responded wholeheartedly to his caresses.

"Infant, I only have so much control," Sean said thickly, burying his face in her neck, his mouth finding the sensitive cord near her ear. "I want to make love to you properly and teach you to glow with passion. I want you to be all mine."

A chill crept across her heart. Was that what he really wanted, after all? An affair? Valerie knew she loved Sean, but did she love him enough to overthrow all of her moral scruples and bear the pain when he tired of her?

"You mean you want to sleep with me after all," she stated huskily. "You want me to become your mistress."

He smiled faintly at her flat statement. "Yes, I want to sleep with you, but not as my mistress. As my wife." He stressed the last word, letting the meaning sink in. "I love you, Val, and I don't want to lose you. I know I'm a lot older than you are and that you have so much ahead of you. I'm only an army engineer, sent wherever they need a bridge or a dam built. I don't have much to offer you."

Valerie's eyes shone as she looked at his face. Sean wanted *her!*

"This wasn't the way I had intended to propose to you," he said wryly. "I wanted to give us more time together, to let you find out about your feelings. But after seeing Anne's treatment of you tonight and the way other men looked at you . . ." His voice roughened with emotion. "I'll teach you to love me, Val. I know you're not indifferent to me."

"Oh, Sean, I love you so much it hurts." Her voice trembled. "I don't care about anyone or anything else but you."

He cupped her face tenderly between his hands, his eyes warm with love. "I don't want you to give up your dancing, Val," Sean said huskily. "You've worked too hard for me to ask you to. But before any of this gets any further, I want to meet your father and ask him officially for your hand."

"My parents were killed in an airplane crash six months ago," Valerie whispered, the painful memory reflected in her eyes.

His arms tightened convulsively around her. "That shows how little we really know about each other," he sighed heavily. "After we get the license we have three days before we can get married. I don't intend to give you enough time to change your mind."

"I won't," she assured him, pressing her lips against his throat.

"First thing Monday we'll apply for the license," he murmured. "I suggest you get plenty of rest, because you won't get much on our honeymoon."

Chapter Three

When Valerie next entered the house overlooking the sea, she was Mrs. Sean Hunter. She nervously twisted the plain gold band and diamond engagement ring that Sean had insisted on buying for her.

Later, she sat at Janine's dressing table, brushing her hair, delaying her return to the living room. The white nightgown with narrow ribbon straps and matching lacy robe suddenly seemed very sheer. She dropped her hairbrush when a knock sounded at the door.

"I'm going to put the car away," Sean called out.

When Valerie heard the front door close, she wandered into the living room, unsure of how to act on her wedding night. She curled up in an easy chair, tucking her feet under her. When Sean reentered the house, he casually began unbuttoning his shirt.

"Think I'll take a shower." He headed for the bedroom, adding wickedly, "Care to join me?"

She flushed hotly, shaking her head rapidly. Valerie rested her head against the back of the chair, listening to the intimate sound of the shower running in the other room. She closed her eyes, feeling her earlier nervousness fade away.

When next she opened her eyes, she was surprised to see Sean bending over her wearing a dark robe, his hair damp from his shower. She focused her heavy eyelids on his smiling face. "You dozed off, love," he murmured, gathering her unresisting form in his arms to carry her into the bedroom.

Drowsily content in Sean's strong arms, Valerie wound her arms around his neck, resting her cheek against his bare chest, revealed between the open lapels of his robe. He had already pulled the covers back on the bed and she was carefully deposited on the cool sheets and her robe deftly removed. He sat on the edge of the bed, cupping her face in his hands, the fingers tangled in her heavy hair as he gazed thoughtfully into her face. Misreading his expression, she felt a moment's fear that he might already regret marrying her.

"Although you look very seductive in that shred of lace, I still feel as if I'd be seducing a child," he muttered, reluctantly releasing her.

Valerie's heart was pounding so loudly that she felt as if the vibrations were rocking the room. She wet her dry lips as Sean switched off the lamp and shed his robe before stretching his hard, lean length next to her. It was not long before her nightgown drifted to the floor next to his robe.

She was unprepared for Sean's passion, but made up

for her inexperience with her willingness to please him. She arched her slim body against his, inviting his caresses, later remembering only brief pain before being transported to the heights of pleasure. Much later, he raised a trembling hand, pushing the damp strands of hair away from her face.

"I'm not very good at this," Valerie's voice quavered uncertainly.

"I'll teach you what you need to know," Sean murmured, pressing her head against his chest.

Valerie pressed her lips against his moist skin, tasting the saltiness and feeling the muscles tense under her touch. His fingers stroked her cheek lightly, moving tantalizingly down her throat. She soon fell blissfully asleep in his arms.

When Sean awoke later in the night, she stirred in his arms, murmuring his name. The touch of his lips was enough for her to turn to him with full love.

Marriage added a new glow to Valerie. The dance school had accepted her as a pupil, and she spent an average of six to eight hours a day in various ballet classes.

When she awoke one Saturday, she discovered a red rose resting on her pillow, the thorns carefully clipped away. She picked up the flower, inhaling the soft fragrance.

"Happy birthday, angel." Sean brought in a breakfast tray and set it on her lap.

Valerie looked down at the wrapped package on the tray. She finally picked it up, eagerly undoing the bright ribbons. She gasped as the opened box revealed the jade pendant she had admired in the jewelry shop at Ghirardelli Square.

"Oh, Sean!" she breathed. "The pendant I saw that first day we were together."

"Matches those cat eyes of yours." He picked up the delicate chain, clasping it around her neck and sealing it with a kiss.

That evening he took her to dinner at a fashionable French restaurant. "Not too much wine for you. I want you sober when I seduce you later," he said wickedly. "It's amazing that after two months of marriage you still blush."

"It's not all that difficult with some of the things you say," Valerie retorted, her eyes sparkling.

"Maybe that's why I love you so much," Sean said huskily. "A little girl one moment, a seductive temptress the next. I never know what to expect."

The wine from dinner left Valerie in a rosy haze. During the drive home, she snuggled up to Sean, raining light kisses on his face. "I never thought I'd say this to any woman, but *please* keep your hands off me."

She giggled, tracing the outline of his ear with her tongue.

"Valerie Hunter." Sean's thick voice betrayed his rapid loss of control.

"All right, I'll be good." She bounced back in her seat, her hands folded primly in her lap, but her eyes were still bright with mischief.

Valerie hummed to herself as she preceded Sean into the house. He walked up behind her, pressing her backward against him, deftly unzipping her dress. She sighed in contentment.

"Now, as to your other birthday present," he muttered, turning her around as her dress slithered to her feet.

Valerie's big change came the day she was told she would be dancing the lead in *Swan Lake* for one of the public performances the school presented. When she arrived at the house late that afternoon, she found Sean there ahead of her.

"Oh, darling, you'll never guess!" She hugged him excitedly. "I have such wonderful news!"

"So do I," he informed her. "A promotion to major and duty in Sydney, Australia. We have two weeks before I have to report."

Valerie was stunned by his announcement. "B-but my school," she said faintly.

"I'm sure you can find a good school over there." He brushed her words aside. "Now, what about your news?"

"I've been chosen to dance the lead in *Swan Lake* for the school's next public performance," she said woodenly, tossing her carryall bag on the couch.

"Well, I'm sure they can find someone else." Sean stood up, taking his jacket off and loosening his tie.

"Sean, this is very important to me," she pleaded.

"I can understand it's important, hon," he said carelessly. "But you won't be here then."

"I—I would be if I stayed here until after my performance," she ventured carefully. "I could come out to join you afterward."

Sean's body stiffened at her words. "And where does that leave me?" he demanded coldly.

"It would only be for a couple of months." Her voice

dropped to a whisper under his icy stare. Valerie had never seen him so angry.

"And if they decide you're good enough to do something else?" he asked harshly, raking his fingers through his hair. "Do I end up an absentee husband that you visit when you have the time?"

She winced at his cutting words. "Sean, I've been studying ballet since I was six years old. This could be the real test for me," she said quietly. "I need to find out if I'm really any good. I have to know."

"That certainly shows what kind of fool I've been." Sean spat the words out angrily. He spun on his heel, stalking out of the house. A moment later she heard the car roar away.

Valerie curled up on the couch, drawing her knees up to rest her chin on them. She didn't want to lose Sean. She loved him too much. More than her dancing, she suddenly realized. She would tell him when he returned.

By late evening he hadn't come home. She slowly undressed and slipped between the sheets, feeling lonely in the large bed. After a time, she drifted off to sleep.

Hours later Valerie was rudely awakened as the sheets were torn back and her body pulled upright. Her nose twitched as alcohol fumes fanned her face. In his wrath, revealed in the silvery moonlight, Sean reminded her of a pirate on a voyage to plunder the seas.

"You belong to me and you'll do what I tell you," he grated, gripping her forearms in a bruising hold. "Don't you forget it."

"Sean, I—" Valerie's words were cut off by his punishing kiss. He ground her lips against her teeth and she cried out in fright as her nightgown was ripped from her body.

Sean ignored her tears as he savagely possessed her, heedless of her cries of pain. Much later, she curled up into a ball, crying softly. The side of Sean she had just witnessed frightened her. He was now sprawled on his stomach, sleeping deeply from the alcohol. As dawn approached, she crept silently out of bed, wincing from the bruises that were now apparent on her body.

Valerie dressed hurriedly in jeans and a T-shirt, throwing clothing into a tote bag. Tears streaming down her face, she penned a note, propping it against the lamp on Sean's bedside table.

> Sean,
>
> I cannot live with someone who demands submission and punishes if it isn't given. Therefore, all I can do is leave you. It would be better for both of us.
>
> Valerie

She left the house, walking down to the bus stop to take the first bus into the city.

Valerie rented a small room and attended her ballet classes, half-fearing and half-hoping Sean would appear. As the weeks passed, she became more despondent, until one day she fainted in class. After a doctor's examination and his announcement that she was pregnant, she packed her bags, unsure of where to go. Crossing her fingers, she called Sean at the army base, only to learn that he had left the country. Even though she was given a military address where she could contact him, her pride now refused to let him know about the baby.

Unable to dance, Valerie attended secretarial school for as long as she was able. After bearing a son, she contacted Shelly, now living in Phoenix, and left San Francisco to make a new life for herself and her son, Michael.

Bringing her thoughts back to the present, Valerie was unable to fall asleep until dawn. When she did awake late that morning, her eyes burned from her tears. She sat up when Shelly walked in with a cup of hot coffee.

"You look as if you need this." She sat on the side of the bed, handing the cup to Valerie.

"Thanks." She sipped the hot liquid gratefully.

"Dare I ask how the party was?" Shelly glanced at the bruises on Valerie's forearms.

"Sean was there," she said flatly.

"What!"

Briefly, Valerie related the previous evening's events, including the punishing kiss on the terrace.

"How do you know that Sean was the one?" Shelly asked.

"Because it would be a perfect way of humiliating me." Tears streamed down her face as her mind relived those horrifying moments. "To hurt me."

Shelly turned at the sound of the phone ringing. "Sounds like Craig's ring." She grinned.

Valerie panicked, knowing she couldn't speak to him then.

"I don't want to talk to him," she said tersely.

Shelly studied her friend's pale face.

"All right," she said quietly. "If it is him, I'll tell him you're still asleep."

"Oh, Shell, what would I do without you?"

"You'll find out soon enough when I marry Greg," she said lightly, running into the living room. A few moments later she reentered the room with a strange expression on her face. "It's Sean. He wants to speak to you."

"No!" she said vehemently.

"Val, you should at least speak to him," Shelly insisted quietly.

Valerie's unrelenting expression was her answer. Shelly sighed as she walked back to the phone. Valerie got out of bed pulling a cotton robe around her. She was brushing the tangles out of her hair when Shelly came back into the bedroom.

"I told him you were asleep, but he didn't believe me." She shrugged her shoulders. "He said that you won't be able to hide from him forever. And you know he's right."

"I'll go check on Michael." She chose to ignore her friend's words and left the room.

She was surprised as Monday passed and Sean still had not tried to contact her again. Oddly, she felt disappointed at his silence and idly wondered what he was doing. Valerie sighed as she realized she had misspelled several words and would have to retype the letter. She quickly inserted a fresh piece of stationery in the typewriter and her fingers flew over the keys.

When Valerie arrived home, Mrs. Roberts, the baby-sitter, was in the living room, knitting. After she left, Valerie shrugged off the pale blue jacket that matched her button-down skirt. A quick glance told her that Michael was still napping. She went into the kitchen for a glass of iced tea and had just filled her glass when the doorbell rang.

"Now who?" she muttered crossly, going into the living room. She was shocked when the opened door revealed Sean's tall figure. She quickly tried to close it again, but he anticipated her move, pushing past her.

"Why are you here?" she finally managed to choke out.

"I knew that if I phoned you again you'd just hang up on me, so I decided to come over, instead," he said grimly. "Well, aren't you going to offer me a drink? It's hot out there."

"We only have iced tea," she said ungraciously, willing her trembling body to be still.

"We?" He glanced around the simply furnished living room. "I thought Craig lived across town."

"You would think that!" Valerie lashed out angrily. "*Shelly* and I share the apartment."

Sean shrugged his shoulders indifferently. "I believe you offered me iced tea?"

Gritting her teeth, Valerie went into the kitchen. Suddenly she realized that Sean still didn't know about Michael and was thankful that none of his toys were lying around the living room as they usually were. Automatically, she dropped two teaspoonfuls of sugar into the glass.

When she came back into the living room, Sean was standing near the sliding glass door that led to a small balcony. Dressed in light tan slacks and a dark brown short-sleeved shirt, he looked just the way she remembered him. Seeing his profile, she noticed a light sprinkling of gray along the temples of his rich brown hair. His features were harder and more cynical than she remembered.

"Here's your tea," Valerie said huskily, beginning to fall under his old spell.

When Sean turned toward her, his eyes were cold and mocking. He appeared amused by her attempts to give him the glass without touching him. He was surprised by the change in her, from the sophisticated woman he had seen at the party to the tired young woman he saw now. His keen eyes noted the apparent strain in her face and the circles under her eyes. His first reaction was to carry her out of this place and make violent love to her, demanding the passionate response he remembered so well. Yet he also remembered the note she had left him, and his features hardened to granite.

Valerie watched the play of emotions across his face and felt sick as he looked at her with something close to disgust in his eyes.

"You don't mind if I sit down, do you?" Sean asked quietly, implying that he would, whether she wanted him to or not.

"Why have you come here, Sean? To humiliate me more than you did at the dance?"

He noticed a fleeting look of fear in her eyes. Fear of what? Him? The thought sickened him.

"I only danced with you, Val. I didn't rape you," he drawled. "How that could humiliate you is beyond my understanding."

"You know very well I mean the way you practically molested me in the garden!" She choked back a hysterical sob, not wanting him to see her cry. "Did you have to prove that you were so much stronger than me with those caveman tactics?"

Sean's jaw hardened as her words were flung at him. "It seems you're accusing the wrong person," he said coldly.

"There wasn't anyone else there who would have had any reason to do such a disgusting thing." Valerie ignored the icy lights in his eyes as she faced him, her fists clenched tensely against her sides. "Why can't you just leave me alone? Everything between us is dead."

A flicker of something unreadable passed over his face, then disappeared. Sean's hand reached inside his shirt pocket, carelessly dangling a glittering object from his fingertips. Valerie recognized it immediately as her jade pendant.

"I found it Saturday night at the club and recognized it as yours. I had thought you might like it back." He dropped it back into his pocket. "I guess I was wrong."

She felt like crying, because she treasured his birthday gift more than she could let him know. There was pain in her eyes as she looked up. "How did you know where to find me?"

"The phonebook is very handy for that kind of thing," Sean replied. "I thought we should settle a few things."

"Meaning a divorce?" She suddenly felt bleak as she said the words.

"If that's what you want," he said harshly. "You know very well I can't stop you. I'm sure your boyfriend will arrange everything for you. Probably give you a good deal regarding the fee, too."

"Craig is not my boyfriend," Valerie retorted. "He's my boss, and sometimes we go out, but that's all."

Sean's eyes traveled over her figure with studied insolence. "Even though you're skinnier than you used to be, I'm sure Craig is able to see beyond your typing and shorthand skills," he sneered.

Unthinking, Valerie's hand shot out, intending to hurt him physically the way he was hurting her mentally. By the time it reached its target, her wrist was held by a steel vise, hurting until she cried out in pain.

"I ought to—" His threat faded as he looked over Valerie's shoulder, staring as if he couldn't believe his eyes.

She started to speak when a small voice startled her. "Mommy." Michael stood in the doorway of the small hallway rubbing his eyes.

Valerie paled as Sean's dark eyes burned through her. She stepped backward, fearing his wrath. Sean stared at the small boy, who looked up with interest.

"Hello," Michael said cheerfully.

Sean's eyes turned back to Valerie. He swore under his breath so that Michael didn't hear him. "I could kill you for this."

Sean spun on his heel, striding toward the door. Then he turned back toward her. "You can forget about any divorce," he said grimly.

As he opened the door, Shelly was standing on the other side. Her smile disappeared as she saw his angry face. He walked past her without a word. Shelly took in Valerie's pale face and Michael, behind her, and everything fell into place.

"Sean—please wait!" She slammed the door on a startled Valerie and ran after Sean.

He stopped, his back still ramrod-straight as he turned to face her. "Why didn't you tell me?" he demanded.

"How? Send you a telegram saying, 'Congratulations, you have a baby boy, eight pounds, nine ounces.'? As it was, if Valerie had known I kept in contact with you, she would have disappeared, baby and all."

" 'Baby!' That was a small boy in there."

"He's *your* son, Sean," she told him. "You can't deny it."

"Really! *She* accuses me of practically raping her at the party, and now you act as if I'd try to deny someone I never even knew about." Sean wearily closed his eyes.

"Was it you last night?" Shelly asked him.

"She said it was me, so it must be true," he said bitterly. "I don't know exactly what I've done, but it must be a hummer. I'm sure that you think the same. You're her friend."

"I don't care what she thinks. I want to hear it from you. And no matter what you say, I'm not going to repeat any of it to Val," she promised.

Sean sighed as he looked out a large window facing a swimming pool, wearily rubbing the back of his neck. "No, it wasn't me," he said flatly. "What was I supposed to have done?"

"I didn't think so," Shelly replied. "But it will take some heavy convincing for Val to believe it. The incident upset her a great deal." She went on to explain what had happened. Sean's face grew darker as she told the story.

"I'm sure Craig Saunders will console her," he sneered.

"Then I suggest you do something about it," Shelly

said crisply, "before Val feels that Craig is all she has, except for Michael. I have plans Friday, and Val's teaching my seven o'clock ballet class that night. It might be a good idea for you to stop by." She turned to leave.

"Does she care for Saunders?" Sean's quiet voice carried to her ears as she reached her door.

"If she does, it's awfully strange that she cries out for you in her sleep," Shelly said instantly. "Figure it out for yourself."

When Shelly reentered the apartment, Valerie was seated tensely on the couch obviously waiting for her return.

"Why did you go after him?" she demanded, her green eyes blazing with anger.

"I wanted to find out something for myself." She walked into the bedroom with Valerie at her heels.

"He saw Michael. He must realize that he's his son!" Valerie sounded hysterical. "He's going to want to take him away from me!"

"Did he tell you that?" Shelly asked her calmly.

"He was too shocked when he saw Michael. I thought he was still asleep when Sean came. I just know he'll try something to get even," she said bleakly. "I know he must hate me."

"Did you happen to notice that Sean is still wearing his wedding band?" Shelly asked. "Don't you think that's a little strange for a man who seemingly doesn't care?"

"It would protect him from a girl wanting to get too serious," Valerie mumbled, flushing.

Shaking her head at her friend's bitterness, Shelly walked toward the bathroom. "I'm going to take a shower."

Valerie walked back into the living room, looking around at the gold tweed couch and gold velvet chairs she and Shelly had bought at a furniture warehouse sale. Houseplants in colorful macramé hangers were scattered around the room. Sighing, she walked into the smaller bedroom, where Michael was back in bed looking at a comic book. He flashed her a sunny smile. "Who was the man, Mommy?" he asked curiously.

"An old friend, darling." She smiled faintly, sitting on the edge of the bed.

"Does he have a little boy, too?" Michael asked innocently.

Valerie's eyes filled with tears as she reached forward, hugging the small boy tightly.

"Yes, oh, yes, he does," she whispered tautly, resting her chin on his golden-brown hair.

Valerie was surprised by Sean's silence over the next four days. Craig was irritated by her absentmindedness, and every time the phone rang she jumped, afraid it was Sean.

"Valerie, I don't know what the problem is, but this letter is totally unacceptable." He threw the paper on her desk. "If it's possible, I would like to get this out today."

She muttered angrily under her breath as she inserted a fresh sheet of stationery into the typewriter and began typing rapidly.

Friday night, Valerie refused Craig's dinner invitation, explaining that she was teaching one of Shelly's ballet classes that evening. She rushed home to pick up Michael and to change into leotards and tights.

While Michael sat in a corner of the large room, happy with a coloring book and crayons, Valerie was busy teaching the fundamental steps to six women. Concentrating on the complex steps, she soon resumed her former grace.

After the class ended, Valerie glanced over to her sleeping son. Arching her back, she walked over to the stack of records next to the record player, sifting through the albums. She lifted one out, studying the label before placing it on the turntable. After setting the needle on the record, she walked back to the center of the room, her profile reflected in the mirrors along the wall. Her eyes closed as her feet automatically placed themselves in the fifth position, heel against the toes of the opposite foot. The soft strains of a valse from *The Sleeping Beauty* drifted through the air.

Valerie was transported back in time to the day she had auditioned for admittance to the academy. The steps came back to her as if she were still practicing daily. She had danced with all her heart only to walk outside that day and lose it to the dark enigmatic man waiting for her, a man whose touch stirred newly awakened senses to such a fevered pitch that she could only be aware of his hard, lean body against her. As the music ended, she was startled out of her dream world by the sound of hands clapping slowly and steadily, the sound a mockery.

"Very nice." Sean stood in the doorway. "Is that what won you the coveted scholarship?"

"Yes." She felt both angry and confused at seeing him so unexpectedly. "How did you know I was here?"

"Instinct." He entered the room, looking around until his gaze fell on the sleeping boy. "Isn't it a little late for him?"

"He likes coming," Valerie said defensively, turning off the phonograph and picking up a wraparound skirt. "You still haven't told me yet why you're here."

"I thought we could have dinner together and talk," Sean said coolly.

"Michael's too tired and he'll just be cranky." Her tone was just as icy. "Some other time."

"Get someone to watch him."

Valerie looked up with a mutinous expression. "We have nothing to discuss."

"Yes, we do." Sean's eyes flickered toward the sleeping Michael.

Valerie felt a cold rush of fear. "There's a neighbor who baby-sits for me. I can ask her," she said slowly, stooping down to pick Michael up, not wanting to awaken him. Before she could reach him, Sean had come up and easily picked the boy up in his arms. Michael stirred and drowsily looked at the tall man.

"Hello," he mumbled sleepily.

Sean looked down at him with a tender expression. As he looked up at Valerie, his features hardened. "Where's your car?" he asked brusquely.

Valerie turned off the lights in the classroom and led the way down the small hallway. After locking the front door, she headed for her Fiat. Sean carefully laid Michael on the passenger's seat.

"I'll follow you to your apartment." He turned,

walking toward a silver Mark V. Valerie grimaced at her car as it sputtered when she turned the key. Then the car roared to life.

On the road, she could see the headlights of the big car behind her, making sure she didn't escape. Michael sat up in the seat, rubbing his eyes.

"Who's the man, Mommy?" he asked.

"A friend," she said carefully, unsure of how to tell him Sean's real identity. "He and I are going out to dinner if Mrs. Rogers can stay with you." Valerie pulled into the parking lot, with the silver car following close behind.

Sean walked up to the car as Valerie got out. "Well, so you decided to wake up." He looked down at the now-alert Michael.

"Can't I go with you and Mommy?" he begged. "I promise I'll be good."

"Next time," Sean promised. "Funny thing, your mother forgot to tell me your name."

"Michael."

Sean looked over at Valerie's pale face. "Michael?" he questioned softly.

"All of my name is Sean Michael Hunter, Jr," Michael said proudly, unaware of the tension between the two adults. "I'm named after my daddy." He jumped out of the car, skipping toward the entrance, then breaking into a run for the stairs.

"Michael, be careful," Valerie called after him, anxious to break the tension.

Sean's steely grip held her back. "You have a lot to make up for, lady," he said through clenched teeth. "It's ironic that you wouldn't tell me about my son, yet you named him after me."

She wrenched her arm free, her green eyes blazing with anger before walking ahead of him. At the apartment door, Sean took her key, inserting it into the lock and opening the door.

"Go get your pajamas on and brush your teeth," she told Michael before turning to Sean. "I'll be in in a few minutes." He merely nodded as he sat on the couch, looking entirely at home.

Valerie quickly made a phone call to Mrs. Rogers, who told her she'd be over in twenty minutes. Val had been tempted to tell Sean she couldn't find anyone to watch Michael, but she knew he wouldn't let her escape so easily.

Since he was dressed in casual slacks and shirt, she chose a pair of powder-blue slacks and a cream-colored shirt with faint blue stripes running through it. She quickly freshened her makeup and ran a brush through her dark hair. After quickly spraying some perfume around her, Valerie walked into the living room, surprised to see Michael, in his pajamas, sitting cross-legged on the couch talking animatedly to Sean. He turned around, grinning at his mother.

"I brushed my teeth," he informed her. "He has the same name as me." He pointed to Sean.

"As *I*, and don't point," Valerie corrected. "I suggest you get into bed—now."

Michael slid off the couch and turned to Sean, his small hand outstretched. "Good night," he said solemnly.

"Good night, Michael," Sean said gravely.

Michael then walked to his mother, arms out for a kiss, before going into his bedroom. Valerie was relieved when the doorbell rang, dispensing with the need for any conversation with Sean. Mrs. Rogers' sharp eyes looked Sean over, noticing the resemblance to Michael. "Don't worry if you're late, dear." She smiled warmly at Valerie, her eyes still on the handsome man standing nearby. "I have no plans."

Valerie groaned inwardly, reading Mrs. Rogers' thoughts on seeing her with the man who must be Michael's father.

"Thank you for coming on such short notice." She smiled, preceding Sean out the front door.

In the parking lot, he courteously helped her into the car, his touch impersonal. Valerie was surprised by Sean's knowledge of the city as he drove through an older section of town, stopping at a Mexican restaurant famous for its fine food. She had never been there, as Craig, on their occasional dates, preferred to take her to American-style restaurants. Here she could appreciate the quiet simplicity of the low, fat red candles burning at each table and the old-fashioned black-and-white photographs, depicting the early days of the city, on the walls.

When they had been seated, the waitress asked if they wanted drinks before dinner, and Valerie quickly requested a vodka-and-tonic. Sean asked for a particular brand of Irish whiskey. After the waitress took the rest of their order, she left them and Sean laced his fingers in front of him, resting his elbows on the table. "Were you afraid I'd forget you're of age now?" He cocked an amused eyebrow.

"I wouldn't expect you to remember anything at all about me." Her voice sounded calmer than she felt.

A hardening of Sean's features was the only sign that he had been affected by her remark. "You seem to have acquired the look of someone who's been around. They'll believe you're of age," he said cruelly.

Valerie whitened under the ruthless gaze. She began to rise from the table, wanting to be as far away from him as possible.

"Sit down." His tone was that of a man used to being in command.

"I won't stay here to be insulted," she said in a low voice.

Sean leaned back in his chair, lazily lighting a cigarette. "They always say the truth hurts." He spoke briskly. "But that isn't why I brought you here."

"Then why are we here?"

"I suggest we eat our meal first." He spoke calmly as the waitress approached them with their food.

Valerie looked at her chicken enchilada without any appetite. But knowing Sean would not say anymore until after dinner, she attempted to swallow a few bites. There had been times when she had wondered what would happen if he ever appeared in her life again, but she had never thought beyond that. Glancing up under her lowered lashes, she noticed the wide gold band on his left hand. Her hand trembled as she recalled the moment when she had slipped it on his finger. She took a hasty gulp of her drink, letting the alcohol soothe her frazzled nerves. She pushed her plate away, tensely waiting for Sean to finish. He looked up, noticing the faint trembling of her chin.

"When did you cut your hair?" he asked unexpectedly.

"T-two years ago," she stammered, surprised by his sudden question.

"Makes you look younger in some ways." He lit

another cigarette. "Now, as to this cozy family reunion . . ." His lips twisted cruelly.

"It's about Michael, isn't it?" She felt a wave of panic inside.

"How old is he?" he asked.

"Three and a half," Valerie replied, anger beginning to override panic. "What's wrong? Don't you believe he's your son?"

"I'd have to be blind to miss the resemblance." His smile was amused. "So I wouldn't suggest that you try to make me believe he isn't mine. After all, Craig has blond hair."

Valerie gasped at his malicious remark.

"And, as he *is* mine, I should have some say in his upbringing," Sean continued.

"In what way?" She was suspicious.

"He needs a father," he stated coldly.

"He has me; that's enough," she retorted.

"You may be able to soothe a stomach ache or chase away the bogeyman, but you can't teach him to play baseball or show him a man's world," he pointed out—correctly, to her irritation. "You can't do everything for him, Val."

"What you're saying is that you want to take him away from me," she replied in a choked voice.

His dark eyes took in the naked pain on her delicate features. "Not exactly—just that both of us should give him a home." He stubbed out his cigarette in the ashtray. "Let him find out he has a father, too."

"I'd like to go, please." Valerie fumbled for her purse and fled the restaurant before her tears could fall.

In the parking lot, her taut nerves threatened to

break as she waited beside the car. Sean unlocked the passenger's door and helped her in before walking around to the driver's side. He slid behind the wheel, then turned, reaching out to grip her chin, jerking it roughly until she faced him. Green eyes stared into brown ones, a small animal mesmerized by a larger one ready to attack. Sean's fingertips caressed her jawline and moved sensuously along her throat. Valerie trembled under his touch as his fingers tightened convulsively around her throat.

"How does Saunders make love, Valerie, my sweet?" he mused, tightening his grip until tears sprang from her eyes. "Do you curl up to him in the middle of the night? Or utter those throaty moans of joy as he possesses you?"

"Do you enjoy abusing women, Sean?" She finally managed to choke out the words. "Does it turn you on?"

A look of disgust appeared on his granite features as he released her so suddenly she flopped back against the seat. He turned, flicking on the ignition, silently driving her back to her apartment. She tried to make a hasty escape, but his reflexes were faster than hers. He was out of the car and at the passenger's door by the time she unbuckled her safety belt.

"Thank you for dinner," Valerie said stiffly. "But you don't need to come up with me."

"We still have a few more things to get settled." The steel grip on her upper arm brooked no argument as he escorted her upstairs.

Mrs. Rogers took in Valerie's pale, strained face as the couple entered the apartment. "He's asleep." She smiled warmly, picking up the rolls of fluffy yellow yarn and her silver crochet hook. "I'll be saying good night." She let herself out quietly.

"Would you like some coffee?" Valerie asked tautly.

"No. Just sit down and listen like a good little girl."

She perched on the edge of the chair farthest away from Sean. The corners of his mouth quirked in amusement as he saw her reluctance to be near him. Sean sat on the couch, his hands clasped loosely between his legs.

"I might as well just come to the point," he said crisply. "What you did—not telling me about Michael—is inexcusable. I won't tell you my exact feelings about it because I don't like to use that kind of language to a woman. But you're going to make up for it—in spades."

"Make up?" Her voice was faint.

"I want my son." His announcement sent icy flashes through her body. "But as I know you'd try to fight me every step of the way, you'll have to come, too." Sean's dark gaze settled on her shocked features. "I have a house outside of town, and there's plenty of room there for him to run around and play and do whatever else little boys do."

"And if I don't consent to your so-called idea?"

Sean's eyes traveled around the small living room, noting the slightly shabby furniture. Valerie clenched her hands under his appraisal. It was obvious from the well-tailored clothes and gold watch he wore that he had few monetary problems.

"If not, then I'll take you to court to get custody of him," he stated coldly.

"He's just a little boy, not an inanimate object. He

has feelings, too. I can't just let him go with you. He doesn't know who you are!"

"That's your fault, not mine!" he informed her tersely. "That's why *you* have to come along, too."

"I have a job!" she protested. "Besides, you don't want me. You only want Michael." Her words ended in a faint whisper that held a touch of wistfulness. Valerie kept her eyes on her clenched hands to avoid seeing the cold truth visible on Sean's face. "It wouldn't work out," she said flatly.

"Then what about a compromise?" he suggested. "A six-month trial. After that, if you want your divorce you can have it, and you'll be well provided for. But I want custody of Michael. Or you can stay with Michael and play the roll of a well-adjusted wife without any complaints."

"To protect you from adoring females with big ideas?" Her mouth twisted bitterly.

"Val, I'll have Michael one way or the other." His eyes narrowed to slits. "So what is your answer?"

"I-I'll have to think it over." She stumbled over her words as she rubbed her forehead agitatedly.

"You think it over. You just do that." Sean rose to his feet with the lithe grace of a jungle cat. "And by next weekend be prepared to move into my house." He walked toward the door.

His highhanded tactics made Valerie bristle with anger. Her head rose to face the man she now considered her enemy. Her green eyes narrowed to emerald slits as she also rose to her feet and walked toward the door.

"Tell me, Sean—" her tone was sarcastic—"do you still wear your wedding band so that your girl friends can't get serious? It must be a wonderful form of protection. You know what I mean—'I'm sorry darling, but I have a wife already.'" She kept on ignoring the danger signs emanating from his rigid body.

"Of course, you didn't let yours stop Saunders from climbing into your bed," he sneered.

Unthinking, Valerie's hand shot out, slapping Sean across the face. For an electric moment she stared horrified at the red marks her fingers had left against the tanned skin of his cheek. With a harsh exclamation he roughly pulled her against him, his lips savagely bruising her soft mouth.

"No!" she gasped as his surging mouth punished hers.

"This is exactly what you deserve," he muttered against her mouth, his hot breath fanning her flushed face.

The punishing kiss brought back memories of the incident at the dance, and Valerie began to panic. She frantically struggled in his iron embrace, feeling waves of fear course through her body. She wanted to cry out in protest against his punishment. Sean took his time, ruthlessly plundering her mouth, robbing the sweetness within. Her tears flowed freely when he finally lifted his head and released her.

"I'll be here a week from tomorrow at ten. I suggest you and Michael be ready." A thread of steel was evident in his voice. "Otherwise, be prepared to face the consequences."

"Oh, yes, I know your method of punishment only too well," she whispered, not seeing a strange look pass over his face as he began to stretch out his hand, which he hastily drew back, as if regretting his impulsive action.

"None of your disappearing tricks, either," he added as he opened the door. "I'm becoming well versed in your little tactics."

After Sean left, Valerie childishly wiped her tears away with the back of her hand. She walked into Michael's bedroom as he sat up in bed, rubbing sleepy eyes with his fists.

She sat on the edge of the bed, facing him. "Michael, Sean has a very large house near here and would like us to live there with him. Would you like that?"

"Why?" He posed to his favorite question.

"B-because he's your father, Michael." She cursed herself for telling it so bluntly. "He wants us all to be together."

The small boy appeared to study his mother's tense features. "Can I take my bear with me?" He referred to his favorite toy.

"Of course you can." Valerie laughed, hugging him before she tucked him in and went thoughtfully into her own room.

Sometime later, still awake, her mind drifted, remembering the intense virile man she had tried, in her own naïve way, to know. Painfully, she wondered how much Sean remembered of that last night they were together. She shivered, remembering the savage passion he had displayed toward her as he cruelly used her to prove his dominance. Young and unexperienced, Valerie had not known that it had been injured male pride and alcohol that had turned him into a vengeful animal. Fearing his anger, she had fled. His manner through most of tonight and at the dance showed her he hadn't changed. Yet, sometimes tonight, he had seemed different. Even though she had panicked under his punishing kiss, tiny flames of desire had begun to burn. Moaning softly, she wrapped her arms around her body, soon falling into a deep sleep and not even waking up when Shelly came in much later.

The next morning, Valerie was awakened by a soft and furry object tickling her nose. Opening her sleep-filled eyes, she gazed into two green ones filled with laughter.

"Shelly said I shouldn't talk too loud or I'd wake you up," Michael whispered. "So I let my bear wake you up, instead. She didn't say he couldn't."

Chapter Four

Valerie laughed, kissing him soundly on the cheek. "And thank you for such a lovely way to wake up." She playfully rubbed her nose against his.

"Hey, buster, your breakfast is on the table." Shelly stood in the doorway. "You wait too long and it will get cold." She raised her eyebrows questioningly toward Valerie. "Michael said his father was here last night."

She nodded her head yes.

"What happened?" Shelly asked.

"I'll tell you when my 'hears all, tells all' goes out to play." Valerie got out of bed, pulling on her cotton robe. "He has a habit of repeating all the wrong things."

Shelly chuckled. "Take your time getting dressed. I'll

make sure that he gets at least half of the food in his stomach and not on the floor."

As she had done many times before, Valerie silently thanked her stars for a friend like Shelly. She had taken Val in without questions and helped her throughout the hard times when she was trying to find a job and someone to take care of Michael. Mrs. Rogers had taken care of Michael since he was three months old and treated him as if he were one of her own grandchildren.

After hurriedly showering, Val brushed her hair and dressed in shabby jeans and an old cotton sleeveless shirt. Devoid of makeup, she resembled a teen-ager more than a mother of a young child.

After Michael finished his breakfast and left, ostensibly to put his toys away, Shelly turned to Valerie. "Well, what did Sean want?" she asked bluntly.

Valerie told her of the events of the previous night, leaving out only the absence of love in the reconciliation. Her pride refused to let anyone know that if Sean could have it any other way he would take only Michael and have nothing to do with her.

"You don't look very happy about it." Shelly eyed her sharply.

"It's been a long time." She shrugged her shoulders, attempting to act indifferent. "I'm just not sure of my feelings, that's all."

Shelly shook her head in disbelief as she poured herself more coffee. "It sounds as if the two of you have decided to battle over Michael," she said perceptively. "And for his sake, I hope that's not what it is."

"You'll be getting married next year. Besides, Michael would be better off with a yard to play in," Valerie muttered. "And Sean seems to have the money to afford one."

"There's an item in the paper today about a new engineering firm owned by Sean Hunter and another man, Dave Eastman." Shelly tapped the newspaper with her finger. "You might be interested in reading it." She rose from the table and headed for the kitchen, carrying her dirty dishes.

Valerie watched her leave the room before furtively glancing at the article. Her face burning, she read about the new firm and its two owners. She concentrated on the paragraph about Sean Hunter, who would be living with his wife and son on the outskirts of town. "Mrs. Hunter and their son have been residing in Phoenix for the past few years."

How dare he! She clenched her teeth, angrily crumpling the paper in her hand and pushing it to the floor.

The fighting glow was still in Valerie's eyes later that day when she left with Michael to walk to a nearby park. Michael was content playing on the slides and climbing bars while Valerie lounged on the grass nearby with a paperback book, idly sipping a can of Coke. She smiled, watching her son climb on the monkey bars. Convinced that all was well, she turned to her book. Engrossed in the story, it took some time for Valerie to realize that the high-pitched squeals coming from the other side of the playground were Michael's. Taking her sunglasses from the top of her head and slipping them on her nose to shield her eyes from the bright afternoon sun, she looked over toward him. Her green eyes widened in surprise to see him happily throwing a ball to a casually dressed Sean, who carefully threw it back to him. The small boy looked toward her, waved, and ran over.

"My dad's here, Mom!" he shouted excitedly, braking to an abrupt stop in front of her.

"Yes, darling, I see," Valerie said tensely, looking up at the tall figure walking slowly behind Michael. "Don't tell me you just happened to be in the neighborhood."

"No. I went by your apartment and Shelly said you were here," he replied, sitting down on the grass next to her.

"I'm gonna get a drink of water." Michael ran toward a nearby drinking fountain.

"I never saw so much energy in a kid." Sean laughed softly, lying back and propping himself on his elbows. "Does he ever stop?"

"Only to eat and sleep." She began to relax at his impersonal comments. "And even then not for long."

Reaching near her thigh, he picked up her can of Coke, brushing the denim material of her jeans with his fingertips. He felt her flinch from his light touch. Under her angry glare, he lazily drank from the can where her lips had been only a few moments before, and the casual gesture seemed as intense as an intimate caress to Valerie's raw nerves. Sean wiped his mouth with the back of his hand, keeping his gold-flecked eyes on Valerie's averted face.

"Right now you look more like his older sister than his mother," he said softly. "I guess you were a child bride, at that. I wonder if you knew what you were getting into then."

Valerie's hand lifted and her green eyes blazed with anger. Noting her intentions, Sean's hand gripped hers painfully. "You're out of your league, angel." His voice flowed over her like rough velvet. "Just be the amiable wife you're supposed to be. And that includes staying out of Craig Saunders' arms."

Valerie opened her mouth, intending to tell him she had no desire to be with Craig, or, as a matter of fact, with him, but snapped it shut, deciding she'd only lose by it. Sean noticed the argumentative expression flash across her face and smiled. Sitting up, he leaned over and, with one finger, turned her chin toward him. Her eyes were the color of dark emeralds, a sure sign of her anger.

"People will think we're arguing if you keep on looking at me that way," he told her lightly.

"Let me go, Sean," she said tensely.

He released her face and resumed his lazy position. "You're free."

"No, I mean let me *go*. You don't want me anymore, so why should we pretend to reconcile?" she asked as the knots tightened in her stomach. "It's not to your advantage."

Sean's features turned to stone. "The reason is over there on the slide," he replied icily, gesturing toward Michael. "I want to get to know the son you selfishly chose not to tell me about. I suggest you put a smile on that sulky face because he's coming this way." He picked up the romance she was reading, leafing idly through it. "It seems you believe the world is a fairy tale and you're just waiting for your handsome prince. Grow up, Val, or your son will first."

"I hate you for this." Her low voice wavered.

"Then we're even, my love." The cold expression he

presented to her warmed as Sean looked up at his son. "Hey, pal, slow down; you have the rest of the afternoon ahead of you."

"No, he has to take a nap soon." Valerie jumped unsteadily to her feet.

"Maybe he'd rather go for some ice cream first?" Sean suggested, which brought a squeal from an excited Michael.

Valerie hesitated, wanting to stay as far away as possible from Sean.

"You can leave your car here and we can all go in mine," he told her, his tone politely mocking. "And if you're afraid, you can sit in the back seat."

"Mommy can't leave our car here because we walked here," Michael piped up. "The car makes funny noises." Valerie flushed under Sean's sharp gaze.

"Can I have chocolate ice cream?" Michael looked up at his father, his dark green eyes shining. "Two scoops?"

"Two scoops it is, pal." Sean laughed, lifting the small boy in his arms. "And if we ask her nicely, your mom just may have some, too."

Valerie did have ice cream—dark chocolate with coconut cream.

"You've got chocolate on your face." Sean grinned, picking up a napkin. "It seems you're as bad as your son."

She tensed in shock as he gently wiped away the sticky substance from her upper lip. She raised pained eyes to his gold-flecked ones, which darkened as they rested on her slightly parted lips. Valerie was oblivious of the people around them. As far as she was concerned, they were the only ones in the world . . . a private and intimate world she hadn't felt in a long time. Inconsequently, she thought that someone had sprinkled gold flakes in his eyes that glittered only when his emotions were aroused. But what emotion caused it this time? Passion? Certainly not love; maybe it was hate. Involuntarily, she shuddered, fearing the latter. Quickly, she turned to her son. "We have to get you home for a nap, young man."

"I don't need a nap! I'm not tired."

"You will be by the time we get home."

"Aw, Dad, do I have to take a nap?" Michael pleaded, looking at his father.

Valerie felt a pang at seeing how easily Michael had adapted to having a father.

"I think your mother's right about that," Sean said to her relief. "Besides, that will give me more time to talk with her."

Valerie opened her mouth to protest at the casual way he was taking control of her life, then closed it again as she saw his eyes slide down to Michael. She realized anything she wanted to say would have to be said away from Michael.

"I have a lot of things to do today," she said stiffly as Sean unlocked the passenger's door of the car.

"Such as?" he asked casually.

"Washing Michael's school clothes, my things, cleaning the house, and doing some mending," Valerie said triumphantly.

Sean eyed her skeptically as he slid behind the steering wheel. Michael chattered throughout the ride, climbing from side to side of the large back seat.

"Don't put your feet on the upholstery, Michael. You'll get it all dirty," Val scolded, her tone sharper than usual.

"It can be cleaned, Val," Sean said calmly. "He can't hurt anything."

"He still has to learn to be careful with other people's possessions." She bristled at Sean's high-handed way of letting Michael do whatever he wanted.

"Do you have horses at your house?" Michael's question brought Sean's edict back into her mind. "Can I ride one? Can I have a tricycle?"

"Michael!" she reprimanded sharply. "You do *not* go around asking other people for things."

Michael, unused to his mother's anger, sat back in his seat, his lower lip trembling.

"I'm not 'other people,' Val. I happen to be his father." Sean's icy voice brought a flush to her cheeks. "Which happens to make a great difference."

She was grateful when the car pulled into the apartment parking lot and hurriedly flung herself out of the car without a backward glance, leaving Sean to see Michael to the door.

As soon as she had put Michael to bed, Val turned to Sean, her eyes blazing. "It's all your fault! I was doing just fine until you came around. I made a good life for myself and Michael. We don't need you."

"That's what you think," Sean ground out, pulling her against his hard body. His hard mouth punished her soft one and Valerie's head whirled until she thought she would faint from lack of air. When he abruptly released her, she swayed toward him until his words hit her like a shower of cold water.

"That's to remind you who's in charge now. I'll see you next Saturday at ten. And try to look a little more presentable." He spun on his heel, leaving the apartment.

Her anger dissolved any other emotions she might have felt earlier. She picked up a gold velour pillow and threw it against the door. Her first thought was to pack her belongings, and Michael's, and run away. But she knew Sean would be after them like a shot, or rather, after Michael. It was painfully obvious that he cared only for his son and not at all for her.

Val knew that she would have to tell Craig about Sean, but she would put it off as long as possible. Knowing him as well as she did, she doubted she would be able to make him understand, especially when *she* still couldn't understand Sean's motives for this reconciliation.

By mid-morning Monday, Valerie was exhausted. Craig noticed her darkly circled eyes and pale face as she sat across from him, taking dictation. "You look awful. Are you coming down with something? Why don't you and I go out for a long drive this Saturday? Do you good to be away from the kid for a while. Where would you like to go?"

She realized that she had to tell him now.

"I-I can't go anywhere, Craig." Valerie swallowed hard, her eyes on her neatly written steno pad. "You see, my husband is in town."

"Val, that's wonderful!" he said happily, rising from his desk and moving around to take her hands in his. "How did he find you?"

"I don't know. I-I guess he's always lived here, but I didn't know it. He had been out of the country for a long time and just came back a few weeks ago," she said faintly. "I guess he's back here for good now."

"Why didn't you tell me sooner?" he reproved. "We can get the separation papers in the works and you'll soon be a free woman."

"I'm afraid we can't do that, Craig." Valerie's voice was husky. "We—uh—we're getting back together again."

Craig abruptly released her hands and leaned against his desk, a chilling expression on his face. "So you're going back to this man after what he's done to you?" he asked finally.

"I left *him,* Craig." She felt uneasy under his dark gaze. "We need to make a home for Michael."

"I offered you a home—and much more." He gripped her forearms as she rose from her chair and drew her against him.

"Craig, please don't spoil it," Valerie begged, struggling in his embrace, trying to evade his descending mouth.

"If the two of you will excuse me, I came to take my wife to lunch." A cold masculine voice halted Craig's kiss.

Sean stood in the doorway, a grim expression on his face. His gray suit, maroon silk shirt, and striped tie accented his dark good looks.

"So, you're the wandering husband." Craig smiled crookedly at his friend as he released Valerie's arms. "And to think of the two of you, cool as cucumbers at the dance when you 'met.' Or was it all planned?" There was a trace of a sneer in his voice.

"Val didn't know I was anywhere near here," Sean told him in a hard voice, his eyes cold as glass as they rested on Val's flushed face. "And it's obvious that she still intends to play her little games."

Tossing her steno pad on the chair, Valerie pressed her lips tightly together to still their angry trembling. "If you 'gentlemen' will excuse me, I'm going to lunch." Her voice revealed her shaky inner self as she headed toward the doorway, which Sean was still blocking. "Alone." She looked up at his granite features and, surprisingly, he stepped aside to let her pass.

Without turning around, Valerie willed her shaky legs to carry her to her desk, where she retrieved her shoulder bag from a bottom drawer. Moments later, her car was roaring out of the parking lot.

Her appetite gone after the turbulent scene at the office, Valerie finally parked the car at a fast-food restaurant and ordered a soda to wash away the bitter taste in her mouth. Soon, she knew, she would have to return to the office and face Craig. When she finally got back, she was relieved to find him gone, with a note on her desk leaving instructions about the dictation he had given her that morning. Blanking out her mind, she sat down at her typewriter, busily working on the correspondence.

That evening, Valerie began to pack her clothing and sort through Michael's clothes.

"You don't have to look as if you'll be entering Dracula's castle, Val." Shelly sat cross-legged on her bed, her long legs tanned in contrast to her white shorts and T-shirt. "You and Michael will be well cared for."

"Michael does fine now," Val replied curtly, carefully folding her sheer lingerie and placing it in a pile on the bed.

"What about his tonsils? He's been sick a lot lately, and you know they'll have to come out," Shelly gently reminded. "And you don't have enough insurance to pay for it."

"I still have money from that legacy." Valerie referred to money she had received after the death of a distant relative several years before.

Shelly sighed at her friend's stubbornness. "I'm going to get us a couple of sodas." She uncoiled herself from the bed and left the room.

Opening various dresser drawers, unthinking, Valerie opened one of Shelly's. She had started to close it when an envelope shoved in a corner and bearing foreign stamps, caught her eye. Curious, she picked it up, seeing a military post box as a return address. The color drained from her face as she hastily scanned the boldly written contents.

> I have arranged for a lawyer to contact Val stating that she will be receiving a legacy from a distant relative since you've said she's been too ill to work.
>
> I appreciate your keeping in touch with me and letting me know how she is. As per your suggestion, I'll write to you at your school.
>
> Thanks,
> Sean

"Val, I—"

Valerie turned, facing her friend with an accusing expression on her face. "Oh, Shelly, how could you . . . ?" Her strangled whisper could barely be heard. "And to think he claimed no knowledge of Michael!"

"He *didn't* know. Really. I wrote to Sean and told him you were very sick," she explained. "If you look at the date on that letter, you can see it was written after you had come here, when you couldn't find work."

"But you kept on writing him!" Valerie accused.

"He cares for you, Val," Shelly said quietly. "Remember that. If he didn't, he wouldn't have bothered to find out how you were doing."

Those words haunted her for the balance of the week and all through Saturday morning as she was helping Michael get dressed. She was surprised to see how few belongings they really had, and the majority were Michael's toys. She left her furniture behind for Shelly, knowing she and Greg could use it in their new apartment when they married. Sean's only comment as he loaded their few suitcases in the car was an arching of the eyebrows.

Valerie remained silent during the ride, content to look out the window at the far hills painted gold and purple against the brilliant blue sky. Sean shot her a sideways glance but said nothing, addressing his remarks only to Michael, questioning him about his school and playmates. She felt a stab of jealousy that her son could talk so easily to a man he had known for only a week.

"We'll be at the house soon," Sean commented to Valerie.

"That's nice." She appeared disinterested as she concentrated on the view through the window.

"I can see you're excited over your new life." His low voice held a trace of mockery.

"I had a new life, thank you." She also kept her voice low so Michael couldn't overhear their tense conversation. "And I was doing quite well at it."

Sean's mocking gaze took in the shabby jeans and T-shirt she had donned that morning. "Is that why *our* son is wearing shoes that should have been thrown out months ago?" he asked tightly.

Valerie's head snapped around, her eyes fired with anger. "For your information, those shoes are the ones he plays in," she hissed. "It's the only way I can keep his school shoes looking nice. As it was, I didn't realize that my 'legacy' was from you, or I never would have used it."

"I suggest we continue this discussion later, away from half-pint's sharp ears." Sean's deceptively soft voice held a strong thread of steel.

Several minutes after he had pulled off the main road, passing through open white-painted gates, he slowed the car in the curving driveway in front of a large house.

Chapter Five

Valerie's eyes widened in surprise at the sight of the large, sprawling H-styled ranch house. The outside was adobe and it had the traditional Spanish red-tiled roof with a covered archway above the oversized double front doors of carved dark wood. The larger windows, with black wrought-iron grilles over them, had window-boxes in front, adding splashes of brilliant color against the off-white background.

"This is your house?" Her tone was accusing as she faced him.

"That's right," he replied briefly, stopping the car and getting out to open the back door for Michael. "You're home, pal."

While the small boy eyed the house with undisguised interest, Valerie slowly climbed out of the car, feeling as if she had been transported to another world. Her uneasiness increased as she eyed the impeccably landscaped area and the cement driveway winding toward the back of the house.

"How could a mere army major afford a house like *this?*" she asked sarcastically, her arm outstretched toward the sprawling house.

"It's been in the family for years," he explained impersonally. "I'll show you the inside."

"It really doesn't matter." She shrugged her shoulders, trying to appear indifferent. "After all, I won't be here for very long."

Sean shot her a sharp glance before walking toward the front door. "I suggest you watch your words," he murmured, a warning in his voice as he led the way inside. Valerie ignored him, looking around the cool interior of the entryway.

"Sara, we're here," Sean called out toward the back of the house.

"I can hear you all right. I'm not deaf." A cheerful voice sounded from down the hallway. The owner of the voice soon appeared and a pair of shrewd blue eyes examined the new arrivals.

"Val, Michael, this is Sara, my housekeeper." Sean smiled warmly at the older woman. "No matter what, she seems to keep everything running smoothly. Sara, as you can guess, this is Valerie, and this is Michael."

"And about time, too," she said briskly. "The rooms are ready. I suppose you'd better show them around, because I have apple dumplings ready for the oven and I want to get back to my kitchen."

"Then I won't give you any excuse for them to fail," he teased, showing a new side of himself to Valerie.

"I'll take care of the grand tour." He steered Valerie and Michael along a hallway to the right. She noticed several opened doors, revealing obvious guest rooms, until they stopped before a closed door. Sean's hand rested on the knob before opening it. "This is your room, Michael."

"Oh, Mommy," he whispered, looking at the large room with a rocking horse in one corner and bunk beds dominating one of the walls. It was clearly a room meant for a boy.

"Sean, it's too much," Valerie protested, alarmed by Michael's rapt expression. She could feel her son slipping away from her. Jealousy invaded her bones as she saw her son's love transfer to his father. "He's too young for many of those things. I can't allow it."

"*You* can't allow it?" Once again, Sean's soft voice was threaded with steel. "I've been denied my son for too long, and I intend to make up for it any way I can."

She flinched, as if struck, under his icy gaze.

Ignoring her, Sean spoke to Michael. "You stay and look around while I show your mom her room."

At his words, her head shot up in alarm. He had told her they were reconciled in name only. He was going to keep his word, wasn't he? The mockery in his eyes told her that he read her thoughts.

"I'm sure you'll find your accommodations suitable." He gave her a gentle push down the hallway. Her steps faltered as they moved closer to the large imposing doors at the end. Sean stopped at a door on the right just before the double doors.

"The master bedroom," he said drily. "Would you care to see it?"

"No, thank you," she said stiffly.

"Then look at your own room, instead." He opened the door next to them.

Valerie walked slowly inside, charmed by what she saw. The large room was simply furnished; the double bed was covered with a colorful patchwork quilt, obviously handmade. A small round table, covered with the same patchwork print and with a small lamp on top, was next to the bed. There was a large closet to one side and a bathroom along another wall. Windows with colorful curtains and light wood furniture gave the room a bright and airy look. She looked around her, all her insecurities temporarily forgotten as she examined her new room.

"Lunch is at twelve-thirty." Sean coldly broke in on her thoughts before striding abruptly from the room, a strange look in his gold-flecked eyes.

She went over to inspect the beige and blue bathroom and came out to see her suitcases sitting by the bed. She had started unpacking when the door slowly opened to reveal a small figure.

"My dad said you were here." Michael's sudden smile lit up his face. "Are we going to live here now? Where will Shelly sleep?"

"She won't be staying here, darling, just us," Valerie replied carefully, sitting on the bed. "Remember how I explained to you that we would come here to live with your father?"

"Does my dad want us here?"

"Of course he does." She acted as if everything were normal. "Now, let's see if we can find the dining room." She quickly brushed her hair and dabbed on her perfume.

"Dining room?"

"In this house, I doubt very much we'll eat in the kitchen," she said drily.

When Valerie opened her bedroom door, she was surprised to see Sean walking down the hall. Michael squealed with glee at seeing his father.

Sean smiled warmly, the smile disappearing as he turned to Valerie. "I thought you might like some help in finding the kitchen for lunch. We're not too fancy around here."

"Mommy said that in this house she doubted very much we'd eat in the kitchen," Michael parroted.

"Did she, now?" Sean murmured. "Next time I'll have Sara use the best china and the dining room."

"Please, not on my account. After all, I shouldn't get airs above my station, should I?" Valerie's green eyes were frosty as she looked at him.

Walking back toward the front of the house, Sean steered them toward the other side, giving Valerie a quick glance at a large living room and another large room equipped with a console television set, stereo equipment, and a bar. Two long, comfortable-looking tweed couches were against the walls. She even noticed one room designed like a small ballet studio, complete with stereo, mirrors and a practice barre. Sean led them toward a swinging door opening to reveal a well-equipped kitchen. An oblong butcher-block table was in one well-lit corner with dark brown leather chairs around it. Shelves were set along the walls with decorative green leafy plants hanging down. Sara was busy at the stove, barely looking up when the trio walked in the room.

"Everything's ready," she said briskly. " Better get seated."

"Is there anything I could help you with?" Valerie asked, feeling uncomfortable at the idea of being served.

"I run my own kitchen, thank you." Sara's manner was brusque but not unkind. "Would you like coffee, iced tea, or soda? I also have milk."

"Iced tea, please." Valerie sat down at the table, uneasy as Sean sat down across from her.

Valerie was relieved that Michael said nothing about their taco salad of crisp lettuce, tomatoes, cooked hamburger, taco chips and grated cheese, since it wasn't one of his favorite foods, but he ate every bite.

"The house seems unusually designed," Valerie commented.

A mocking look appeared in Sean's eyes, as if he had guessed, correctly, that she was only endeavoring to make polite conversation.

"My father built it many years ago. He and my mother entertained quite a bit and the main part of the house is away from the sleeping quarters. Sara has her own living quarters. Then there's a pool and barbecue in the back."

"A swimming pool!" Michael's eyes lit up with excitement. "Can I go in it?"

"Not without me or your mother," Sean said sternly. "And that's an order."

"I can swim," Michael protested. "I could from the time I was real little."

"Michael was learning to swim before he could walk," Valerie explained. "And his preschool also had swimming classes every year."

"You're not a normal mother, my sweet," Sean said

with deceptive softness, his brown eyes capturing her green ones. "How can you work, spend so much time with our son, and still be able to go out with other men?"

"I didn't start dating Craig until a year ago." She could have bitten her tongue for revealing those years of loneliness, the years when she would wonder where Sean was and secretly hope he'd come back. Now she was past that. He was back, not for her, but for her son—*their* son. So now he would have his revenge on her for not contacting him about Michael. She would be forced to live in his house, to watch her son's love transfer completely to his father. And that would hurt her the most. As these thoughts flickered through her mind, she was unaware that Sean was watching her under his eyelashes as he continued to talk with Michael. Deep in her own thoughts, she was startled to realize that he was directing a question to her while Sara set plates of warm apple dumplings in front of them.

"What? I'm sorry, I guess I was daydreaming," she apologized.

"I asked if you would like to go outside with Michael and myself." His tone was that of an adult speaking patiently to a scatterbrained child.

"I'd like to go back for my car."

"There's plenty of time." Sean shrugged his shoulders, tackling the flaky crust of his apple dumpling and ignoring her once again.

The patio was laid out with a brick barbecue off to one side of the large pool. A curved slide stood near the diving board. Michael ran around excitedly, stopping only to dip his hand in the water.

"Michael, you really should be having your nap," Valerie told him. "It's later than usual for you."

"I'm too big for a nap," he cried stubbornly, but a word from Sean quickly stopped the beginning of a tantrum.

By the time the small boy had changed into his pajamas, he was beginning to droop. He climbed into his bed and Valerie adjusted the covers over him, then left the room, walking down to her own. She was surprised to find Sean seated in the chair near the bed. "What are you doing here?" she demanded.

"You don't need to worry about your precious body," he said sarcastically. "I just wanted to make sure the room was to your liking."

"It's the same as any prison." She shrugged her shoulders.

"It's whatever you make of it," Sean stated flatly, rising to his feet. "Dinner's usually at seven. Would six-thirty be better because of Michael?"

"Why ask my advice? I'm just part of the package deal." Valerie turned away from him.

In a single stride, he was beside her, gripping her arm and spinning her around to face him. "You're really going to be difficult about this, aren't you?" he grated. "I suggest you listen carefully to what I'm going to say because I won't repeat myself. You change your attitude now, or I'll be down on your head before you know what hit you. I'll make you rue the day you ever decided to cross me."

"I already rue the day I ever met you!" she cried out passionately, vainly trying to free her arm. "I wish I had never seen you that first time on the beach!"

"Then that makes two of us!" Sean growled, freeing her arm and stalking out of the room, slamming the door behind him.

When Valerie looked down she saw that her hand was trembling violently. She slowly undressed, letting her clothes drop to the floor in a small pile. She walked into the bathroom and stood under the hot shower, willing her cramped muscles to relax. After drying herself off, she walked back into the bedroom and crawled into bed to fall into a deep, exhausted sleep.

When she awoke later in the day, she wearily pushed her hair away from her face as she turned to glance at the clock. She was surprised by the late hour. It was already six-thirty.

She quickly donned navy pants and a red-and-white striped blouse before brushing her hair into a semblance of order. Afterwards, she peeked into several rooms before finding Sean and Michael in the dining room. Her place was set at Sean's right, but he barely nodded as she seated herself. She began to eat the thin slices of roast beef in front of her.

Valerie was silent throughout the meal, listening to the conversation between Sean and Michael. She felt jealous of their instant camaraderie, of a closeness she couldn't share with her son. A few moments later, the phone rang in the distance and Sara stuck her head around the kitchen door.

"It's that Felicia Everst for you." She looked at Sean, her very manner disapproving.

"Excuse me," Sean said as he rose from the table. "I'll take it in my study, Sara."

Into Valerie's mind flashed the picture of the dark-haired woman who had been by Sean's side at the party. They were certainly more than casual acquaintances, judging by the woman's manner.

"Jealous, love?" Sean's amused voice interrupted her thoughts as he walked past her. "What *is* that old saying? We 'envy what we can't have.' "

She glared at his retreating back, refusing to answer. A moment later, she could hear him warmly greeting Felicia before the study door was pointedly closed.

"I like it here," Michael happily commented, attacking his apple dumpling. "I liked it where we lived with Shelly, but now you have your very own room, Mom. You don't have to share it, do you?"

"No, I don't, do I?" Valerie said, wondering why that thought hurt so much.

Valerie turned, suddenly feeling Sean's mocking gaze boring into her. "I have a business appointment in twenty minutes."

"Fine," she replied indifferently, turning back to her plate.

A hand gripped her chin, jerking her around to face cold dark eyes. "For Sara," he murmured, brushing a light kiss across her lips, leaving them tingling from his touch.

"She's in the other room," Valerie said coldly, keeping her voice low.

"You don't need to wait up for me." He released her chin and straightened up.

"Don't worry, I won't," she retorted, turning back and pretending to stir her coffee, much to his evident amusement. Moments later, the front door slammed and the roar of the powerful car engine could be heard.

Later that evening, after Michael had been tucked into bed, Valerie wandered through the quiet house. Sara had retired to her room an hour before. Feeling too restless to read or watch television, she impulsively decided to take a swim. She quickly changed into a daring white bikini with crochet work along the sides of the narrow briefs and lacy halter top. She brushed her hair away from her face, pinning it on top of her head.

Valerie gasped with delight as she dove into the cool water and effortlessly glided into a sidestroke. She became so engrossed in her swimming that she failed to hear heavy footsteps on the concrete patio.

"Well, well; the water sprite is back." The familiar mocking voice brought her to a standstill. She quickly swam over to where Sean stood at the edge of the pool.

"You frightened me." Valerie laughed nervously, gripping the edge. Her wrists were suddenly gripped by strong hands and she was pulled bodily out of the pool.

"You shouldn't be out here swimming alone." Sean walked with her toward the sliding glass door that led into the den. "There *are* men you should be afraid of."

"Are you one of them?" She seemed to challenge him.

He walked over to the bar, pouring two drinks and handing one to Valerie. "Am I?" Sean asked softly, keeping his hand on the glass as she attempted to take it.

Feeling uneasy under his hooded gaze, Valerie chose to ignore his question and quickly changed the subject. "I'm surprised you're back so early. I thought you wouldn't be back until much later."

"Oh? Why?" He studied her face as he leaned back against the bar.

"I got the impression that Felicia doesn't let go easily," she replied, sipping her drink.

Sean lit a cigarette, his narrowed eyes watching her every move. Valerie wandered restlessly around the room, chattering to hide her nervousness. "This is such a lovely room. It seems to have such a warm feeling," she rattled on inanely, "although I would like to put some plants in here. The light is very good for philodendrons."

"Stop it, Val!" He slammed his glass down on the bar, causing her to jump. She didn't notice the white lines around his mouth.

"Well, I guess I'll go to my room," she said hesitantly, setting her glass down. "Good night."

As she passed him, Sean's hand shot out, lightly gripping the nape of her neck under her damp hair. "You *should* be afraid of me, angel," he said huskily. His fingertips stroked her bare midriff, burning her skin.

"Are you drunk, Sean?" She was surprised to hear that her voice was steady despite the upheaval of her emotions.

"Not drunk enough. Your skin's as smooth as silk." His fingers moved upward to cup her breast, bringing a trembling to her lower limbs. "Do you still sleep all curled up, Val? I used to enjoy watching you sleep in my arms all warm and soft like a kitten. And then you would turn into a passionate tigress, wanting me as badly as I wanted you." His soft voice seduced her senses, sending her swaying toward his hard body.

Sean's thumb rubbed the hollow of her throat and his

lips soon followed. He teased the corners of her mouth, leaving behind an ache for the full possession of his lips.

"Sean," she breathed as his mouth closed fully over hers and she was lost. Valerie moaned softly as his mouth moved sensually over hers. She gripped the front of his shirt, her legs trembling so much that she was afraid of falling.

Sean bent slightly, picking her up in his arms to hold her close against his chest. His lips brushed the top of her hair as he walked out of the room. She closed her eyes as she cushioned her head against his shoulder. His touch was reviving memories that sent hot flashes throughout her body. Moments later, he entered a darkened room lit only by the moonlight streaming through the windows. She felt herself being gently set down on yielding softness and soon Sean was beside her, his body half-covering hers.

"The memory of you like this has been tearing at my guts for four years," he said hoarsely, his lean fingers stroking her slim throat. "The first time I saw you, you were wearing a bikini like this one." He smiled wryly. "The same color anyway, but not as seductive or revealing. If you had, I doubt I would have taken you back to your friends. I wouldn't have been able to let you go."

Valerie's fingers trembled as she unfastened his shirt, spreading her hands against the warmth of his bare chest. She lifted her head to press her lips against his hair-roughened skin.

"Val," he groaned thickly, possessively capturing her lips with his, pressing her down into the soft pillows.

Her arms crept upward around his neck, drawing her closer to him. She felt him unhook her bikini top, pushing it away and kissing her soft skin, bringing a gasp of pleasure to her lips. Her bikini briefs were soon discarded, following Sean's clothing onto the floor. Her hands roamed lovingly over his muscular body. He turned her head as he nibbled her neck, her eyes half-closed. They widened slightly as they noticed his shirt lying on the floor, the moonlight shining on a dark spot near the collar. As she focused her eyes, the dark spot took on a bright red color—a lipstick stain. Valerie never wore red lipstick, but Felicia had—the night of the party.

"It's been so long, Val," Sean said thickly, his hand sensually caressing her bare hip. "Let me love you."

Tears stinging her eyes, she lifted her hands, pushing at his chest. He lifted his head, puzzled by her action. "Val?" His voice was questioning.

"Let go of me," she ordered, her anger giving her strength.

"What the . . . ?" He rolled away from her. "What is wrong with you?" he angrily demanded.

"Oh, very good, Mr. Sean Hunter." Valerie was breathing hard as she stumbled from the bed. "What kind of game is this? Do you think that all you have to do is snap your fingers and I'll jump?"

"What are you talking about?"

"Common sense has finally entered my mind." She blinked angry tears away. "If you think you can come from your mistress's bed straight into mine, then you'd better think again."

A strange light shone momentarily in his eyes as he replied drily, "That would be a little difficult to do, but I won't go into it now. But I *am* wondering what gave you that idea."

"Next time tell her not to blot her lipstick on your shirt!" She gestured wildly toward the floor before running out of the room, blindly heading for her own. She slammed the door behind her, trying to calm herself by taking deep breaths. Her head shot up in alarm when the bedroom door flew open and a glowering Sean entered.

"Don't worry," he ground out, throwing her bikini at her feet, "I wouldn't touch you after that little scene you pulled if you paid me. I don't intend to burn my fingers again." He stalked out, slamming the door. Valerie flew off the bed and flipped the lock shut.

"And if I *were* ever after that body of yours, a lock wouldn't stop me." Sean's mocking tones carried through the door.

Now that Valerie was alone, she was able to let the angry tears fall. She curled up on her bed, hugging her knees to her body, and cried until she was exhausted. Then she stood up, stretching her muscles, and slowly prepared for bed.

She pulled on a nightgown and burrowed under the covers, shivering as if she were very cold. It was some time before she could fall asleep and she tossed and turned all night, muttering restlessly under her breath.

Toward dawn, she awoke feeling more tired than when she went to bed. She felt a keen desire to tire herself out and could think only of one way to do it. She got out of bed and rummaged in her dresser drawer for leotards and tights, quickly pulling them on.

Moments later, she pushed open the door to the room lined with mirrors and a ballet barre. She turned on the stereo after selecting several records and setting them on the turntable in a special order. Standing with her left side to the barre, she began a series of warm-up exercises and stretches to the sounds of the classical music.

An hour later she stopped, feeling hot in her leotard. The damp material clung to her curves, still subtle even after having a child. She carefully replaced the records in their jackets and turned off the stereo before leaving the room.

Back in her room, she could hear Michael's excited squeals and splashing sounds, which indicated he was in the swimming pool. Knowing she couldn't put off seeing Sean too long, she quickly showered and donned a black-and-rust-striped bikini.

Michael was happily jumping off the diving board, while Sean was using a net to snare leaves that had fallen into the pool during the night. Dressed in gold trunks a shade lighter than his deep tan, he made an awesome picture. The expression he gave her was inscrutable as he insolently eyed her bikini.

Taking a deep breath, Valerie strove to act indifferent as she made a clean dive from the edge of the pool and swam its length, enjoying the pull on her muscles. She then floated on her back, unused to having a pool to herself instead of sharing one with both small children and adults, as she did in the apartment complex. After a while, she left the pool for a lounge chair where Sara had set out juice, rolls, and jam.

"How about a couple of eggs?" she asked Valerie, who smilingly refused.

"I'm not really used to eating breakfast," she explained, "although I made sure Michael didn't pick up my bad habit. This is just fine for me, thank you."

"You don't eat enough to sustain a mouse," Sara scolded.

Valerie laughed, the sound clear and pleasing to the ear. Sean looked over at her as if he were unused to her unrestrained laughter.

"You should have seen me when I was pregnant, then," she told Sara, her mouth curved in a smile of remembrance. "I looked like a whale and walked like one, too. I would get the worst cravings for chocolate buttercreams. The doctor used to get so angry at me because I put on so much weight. I had to work hard to get it off after Michael was born. I was so ugly then." Her voice drifted off as her eyes were caught by Sean's from across the pool. His expression frightened her.

"I doubt that very much," Sara replied as she left the patio area. "Pregnant women always have a special glow about them."

Valerie's muscles tightened under Sean's unwavering glance. His eyes lingered insolently on her bare, flat midriff before moving back up to her mesmerized eyes. It was as if he were silently condeming her for not letting him be with her during that precious time. Their tense silence was broken by the sound of a car pulling around to the back of the house. Valerie shivered as she saw Felicia alight from a white Cadillac.

The dark-haired woman was dressed in a red silky sheath with a white braided belt around her trim waist, and her hair was held back by a white folded scarf. Valerie sulkily noticed her red lipstick and the coordinated polish on her long, well-manicured nails. Felicia's cool eyes landed first on Valerie, then moved to Michael, happily paddling in the pool.

"I didn't realize you had company, darling," she purred to Sean.

"Valerie and Michael aren't company." His tones sounded cool to Valerie as he spoke to the other woman. "Val's my wife and Michael is my son."

Valerie was surprised by Sean's cold announcement. Why hadn't he told the woman last night when they were together? Why embarass her now? Felicia's eyes glittered with hatred as she looked at Valerie.

"Congratulations," she drawled. "I guess I should have noticed the coincidence in names and your reactions to each other at the party. Tell me something, were you married recently?" Her eyes strayed over to an unconcerned Michael.

Valerie clenched her hands, trying to control her rapidly mounting anger. "Although it's really none of your business, Michael was born fifteen months after we were married," she said icily. "I don't care what you say about me, but make sure you stay away from him."

"Darling, surely you can understand my feelings about this," Felicia appealed to Sean, her hard eyes suddenly soft and limpid.

"I understand, Felicia." He set the net down on the concrete and approached her, much to Valerie's consternation.

Gritting her teeth, Valerie turned her back on the couple. "Come on, Michael," she said quietly, heading for the house. "I think you should change your clothes now."

"It was nice seeing you again, Valerie, dear." Felicia's condescending tone followed her. "I'm sure we'll meet each other again since Sean and I are such—close friends."

"Yes, of course, Mrs. Everst," Valerie replied politely.

"Felicia, dear." She smiled triumphantly, with Sean standing near her. "No formalities around here."

"I was always taught to respect my elders, *Mrs.* Everst." Valerie smiled, the picture of innocence, receiving an angry glare from Felicia and a look—of what, admiration?—from Sean. "Good-bye."

Inside the house, she sent Michael to change his clothes and walked back to her room.

Valerie spent the rest of the day acting distant toward Sean, much to his evident amusement. *He* spent the rest of the day outside, working on the car engine with Michael avidly watching every move and asking questions. Dressed only in old jeans, Sean's bronze back was shiny with sweat.

Jealously, Valerie watched them from the den window. The man squatted on his heels, his greasy hands holding a car part while he explained its purpose to the interested little boy. Later, when they left to pick up her car at the apartment complex, Valerie didn't volunteer any conversation, preferring the silence, however tense, to a resumption of hostilities.

The following day, Valerie was glad to be able to escape to her office. She quickly showered and washed her hair, then chose a cotton short-sleeved dress with tiny mauve flowers on a cream background. She adjusted the drawstring waist and sprayed on a light perfume.

"Mom!" Michael burst eagerly into the room.

"Michael, how many times have I told you to knock

before entering a room?" she chided, fastening a silver chain around her neck.

"I'm sorry," he said rapidly. "I just wanted to ask if Daddy could take me to school today. Please?"

"Honey, I'm sure he's very busy and—" she broke off, seeing his crestfallen face. "Is there a reason why you want him to take you to school?"

"I just want to show everybody that I've got a daddy, too, just like them," he mumbled, digging the toe of his tennis shoe into the soft carpet.

Valerie's heart went out to him as she drew him into her arms. "Then go ahead and ask him at breakfast."

"Dad, could you take me to school today?" Michael asked as he finished the last of his scrambled eggs.

There had been little conversation during the meal, much to Valerie's relief, as Sean had brought typed reports to the table, studying them as he ate.

"I'm sorry, pal." He glanced up from his reading. "But I have an early morning meeting today. Another day, okay?"

"Okay," he sighed heavily, slipping down from his chair. "Can I be excused, please?" He ran from the room after Valerie nodded. She turned to Sean with flashing eyes.

"For someone who wanted to have his son back so badly, you have a terrific way of showing it!" she hissed, her eyes narrowed like a cat's. "Having you take him to school today was very important to him."

"What's the difference between today and another day?" He was obviously put out by her attitude.

"Because it seems he's told his friends at school that he has a father, after all!" Valerie spat out. "A father just the same as they have. And he wants to show you off!" She threw her napkin down in disgust.

Sean gave her a long look before rising from the table, handsome in a gray suit with a light blue shirt. He left the dining room heading for his study. Valerie sipped her coffee, trying to cool her anger. She could hear Sean's low tones in the study as he spoke on the telephone. Several minutes later she heard footsteps in the hall.

"Michael, if you don't want to be late for school, hurry up," Sean called out.

Valerie quickly rose to her feet and ran to the doorway. Her eyes shone as she gazed at him. "Thank you," she whispered as she watched an excited Michael bolt from his room.

"When possible, meetings *can* be postponed," he informed her, resting a lean hand on his son's shoulder. "See you later."

Michael waved to his mother as he skipped out the front door, and suddenly Valerie had a funny feeling in the pit of her stomach. When she turned around, Sara was standing in the kitchen doorway, watching her.

"I've always taken him to school myself," Valerie admitted sheepishly. "Shelly picked him up sometimes, but I always took him. It feels so strange to see him going off with someone else."

"He's a boy, my dear." Sara picked up the plates. "He'll start turning to his father more and more. It's natural."

"What was Sean like as a little boy?" Valerie asked impulsively.

Sara's face softened as she was taken back into the past.

"Stubborn," she chuckled. "Once he put his mind to doing something, nothing could stop him. Funny, after his mother died, he changed. He grew up suddenly. His father died when he was young and his uncle never knew what to do with kids, so Sean took more care of Janine than anyone. Then as he grew up he became quite a charmer with the girls. Of course, marriage changed that."

"Of course," Valerie said bitterly, turning away.

Driving slowly, Valerie was not too early for work. Seated at her desk, she busied herself sorting various papers to be filed. She was engrossed with her task when Craig walked in, carrying a briefcase.

"Can't wait to get started, can you?" He grinned. "Any messages?"

"Only from Mr. Benson." Valerie's eyes sparkled. At least it looked like Craig wasn't going to be difficult. "He wants to change his will again. He had another fight with his wife."

Craig grimaced at the news. "I had to work on a brief this weekend, so I've got a load of typing for you." His expression turned serious as he noted the faint circles under her eyes. "I know two days isn't long enough to tell, but how are things going so far?"

"Fine." She smiled brightly. "Michael can't get over not having to share a pool with a lot of other kids."

"But what about you?" Craig asked quietly, sitting on the edge of her desk. "Kids adapt pretty easily, but you're the one who counts with me."

"Craig, please don't be this way," she pleaded uneasily. "Sean is my husband, and I have to respect him as such."

"If he's your husband, he has a devil of a way of

showing it," he said fiercely, grabbing her wrist. "Or has he learned how to juggle two women at once?"

"Stop it! Stop it, Craig!" Valerie jerked her wrist away from him. "You have no right to speak to me that way."

"In some ways I have more of a right than he does." Craig stood up. "*I've* always been honest with you." He turned and walked into his office, saying over his shoulder, "And that's more than Sean has ever been."

Valerie rested her shaking hands on the desk, taking deep breaths to calm her jangling nerves.

Craig was a merciless taskmaster that day. He criticized every minute error in her work, insisting that it all be done over. He spent the day in his office grinding out so much work that she was obliged to stay in the office during her lunch hour. By the end of the day, she was ready to drop with exhaustion. She even found it an effort to drive to the preschool to pick up Michael.

At the house, Valerie sent Michael to his room to change his clothes, and she headed for the kitchen for a cold drink.

"Just the two of you for dinner," Sara told her, her sharp eyes noting the tired droop of Val's shoulders. "Sean called and said he'd be late. He wasn't sure when he'd be home. He had a business deal to finish up, he said."

Felicia, Valerie thought to herself bitterly. Some business deal.

"If it wouldn't be any trouble, I'm really too tired for anything except a salad," Val replied. "I'm just too tired to eat anything heavy."

"Why don't you relax in a nice warm tub?" the older

woman suggested. "Do you a world of good. Here, take this with you." Sara handed her a filled wine glass. Her eyes twinkled as Valerie's eyes widened at the large amount. "This will probably relax you more than the bath will."

"I'm sure it will," she replied wryly, accepting the glass. "Or it'll knock me out, at least."

In the hot, scented water, Valerie could feel her tense muscles relax as she slowly sipped the rosé wine and her eyelids began to droop. It was an effort to rouse herself to step out of the tub and dry herself off before slipping on a caftan of bright green cotton.

Michael was quiet during their informal dinner and content to watch television until his bedtime. Then Valerie curled up on the couch, still feeling drowsy from the bath and the wine. She turned on the radio, selecting a classical music station. It wasn't long before her eyelids grew heavy and she soon fell asleep.

Sometime later she slowly awoke, focusing her eyes on the fuzzy figure standing over her. For a moment she was almost certain that his face was soft and tender as he gazed at her. But she must have been mistaken because his features were expressionless as she sat up, yawning deeply. "Wh—what time is it?" She stifled another yawn.

"Just past two," Sean replied abruptly. "Waiting up for me?"

"No, ironically, I fell asleep a little after eight," she snapped, struggling to her feet. "I've had a long day, not half as long as yours, though."

"And just what does that mean?" he demanded, walking toward her.

"Sean, I am still very tired," she said slowly, as if she had to think out each word. "I am going to bed. Good night." She could hear him muttering angrily behind her as she headed for her room. She fell asleep again before her head hit her pillow.

Her days became a pattern. She had been wrong about Craig. He had become cold and distant, a machine, grinding out work each day. Valerie came home bone-weary every night only to discover that Sean would not be home for dinner. Michael seemed disappointed that his father didn't spend much time at home, but he made no comment. The weekends were similar, with Sean rarely home. When he was, he spent his time with Michael and virtually ignored Valerie.

One morning she came into the dining room and found a white envelope on her plate with her name written across the front in familar bold handwriting. Tearing it open, a plastic charge card fell out, along with a note stating:

I requested a card in your name for any purchases you feel necessary for yourself or Michael.

S.

She resisted the impulse to snap the card in half as she read the brief note. Glancing at the card, her mouth twisted bitterly as she read the name printed—Mrs. Sean M. Hunter.

"Someday I'll use this to bankrupt him, if nothing else." She picked the card up. It was obvious that Sean was making it clear that Valerie was his wife, even to the credit card company.

Chapter Six

One particularly hot morning, Valerie chose a light blue cotton dress cut on simple lines. For comfort, she had pinned her hair in a loose knot on top of her head, leaving tiny curls hanging on the sides and the nape of her neck. Since she was later than usual, she was surprised to see Sean at the table reading the newspaper. He was usually gone by the time she came to breakfast. He didn't look up or acknowledge her presence when she entered and poured herself a cup of coffee. Irked by his indifference, she sat down slowly, pouring cream into her coffee.

"Let's get one thing straight," Sean said suddenly, putting his paper down on the table. "Sara is not a servant here; she is not yours to command at your whim."

"I don't command anyone!" Valerie retorted heatedly. "I don't even know what you're talking about."

"What I'm talking about is Sara driving Michael to school."

"I didn't ask Sara to drive him to school," she said slowly, trying to keep a tight rein on her rapidly rising temper. "In fact, she volunteered since she wanted to be in town early today. Of course, I don't expect you to believe me, so you can just ask Sara this evening if you decide to come home at a decent hour. Now, if you don't mine, I think I'll go to work. The atmosphere there is much less confining."

As she left the room, Sean rose to his feet as if to call her back, but then seemed to change his mind and sat back in his chair, a thunderous look on his face.

As soon as she was out of Sean's sight, Valerie ran to her room for her purse and car keys before fleeing the house. She muttered angrily to herself as she went outside and started up her car, revving the engine more than necessary before roaring down the driveway to the private road leading to the main highway. The wind whipped through her hair as she sped down the road toward town. Her anger hadn't cooled by the time she reached the office, slamming file drawers and thrown papers were evidence of her still-flaming temper.

"Hey, that could give someone the impression that you're angry about something," Craig commented, walking into the office.

"He has a lot of nerve accusing me of taking advantage of other people!" she snapped, throwing a manila folder on her desk. "If he keeps up those tactics, he'll be sorry!"

Craig's eyes darkened to a stormy blue. He gripped

her upper arms, pulling her to face him. "Leave him, Val," he said fiercely. "I still want you. You'll never be happy with Sean; I can give you much more."

Except the love I want, Valerie thought to herself sadly.

"There's no reason on earth for you to stay with him," he went on.

"Yes, there is," she sighed. "Please, Craig, I've told you I don't want to discuss it."

His expression was sullen as he released her arms. "You'll always regret this, Val," he said harshly. "I want to give you the world, yet you persist in staying where you're not wanted or loved. You're a fool."

"Then I guess I'll just have to be a fool." She smiled bleakly.

"I just hate to see you this way," he replied. "He has Felicia, and she's all he wants."

Valerie's heart contracted at Craig's statement, knowing it was true. "I still have Michael," she said quietly, sitting down at her typewriter. "And right now, he's all that counts."

Valerie had made plans to meet Shelly for lunch that day, and her attempts to act light-hearted were to no avail. Her obvious lack of appetite had not gone unnoticed by her friend. "Something's wrong, Val, and I think it has to do with Sean," Shelly said bluntly.

"It could be Michael who's bothering me," she said evasively, pushing her salad around on her plate.

"If it were Michael, you wouldn't hesitate to talk about it. So it has to be Sean," she stated logically, then leaned forward, her eyes full of concern for her friend. "Val, I'm not trying to be nosy—please understand that. I only want to help."

The words slowly came out as Valerie briefly sketched her morning argument with Sean. "He didn't even stop to consider that I wouldn't have dreamed of asking Sara to take Michael to school," she sighed. "He just refused to listen to anything I tried to say."

"And, naturally, you immediately lost your temper, lashing out at him instead of trying to calmly explain things. Am I right?"

Valerie nodded.

"Look, I'd love to sit here and have a long chat, but I have a class at two," Shelly said, reaching for her purse.

"My treat." Valerie smiled, throwing a plastic charge card onto the table. "After all, Sean gave it to me for my own use, so why not use it?"

As they left the restaurant, Valerie's eyes were drawn to a tall figure across the street. Her heart sank as she recognized Sean, standing in front of an expensive boutique with a wrapped box under one arm. His head was bent close to a familiar dark-haired one, as if in intimate conversation. Felicia's hand rested possessively on his arm. Val glanced quickly at Shelly to see if she had also noticed the couple, but she was engrossed in finding her sunglasses in her purse. "Just try to keep your temper tonight," she advised, putting her sunglasses on to shade her eyes from the midday glare.

"Oh, yes, I will," Val replied softly, green eyes on the couple across the street.

Valerie's steps faltered as she walked toward her car. She collapsed in the driver's seat, resting her head against the steering wheel. Her eyes were tightly closed against the tears that threatened to fall. Although she knew that Sean was spending his evenings with Felicia, this was the first time she had seen them together since that day at the house.

When she regained her composure she started the engine, putting the car in gear. She was halfway to her office when pictures of Sean and Felicia together passed before her eyes. Fighting sudden waves of nausea, she stopped the car near a phone booth. Taking deep breaths, she unsteadily dialed a number.

"Craig? I'm sorry, but I can't come back to the office." Her voice quavered slightly.

"Val, what's wrong?" he demanded.

"I just can't come back." She felt on the verge of hysteria. "I'll be in tomorrow. Good-bye, Craig." She replaced the receiver in the cradle, cutting off his protests.

Her hands were trembling as she restarted the car and pulled out of the parking lot. Driving through the main streets, she wiped the tears away with the back of her hand.

Caught up in her problems, her reflexes were not as quick as usual. Her tear-filled eyes widened in horror as a large truck in front of her skidded and jackknifed onto its side, spilling its contents onto the road.

"Oh, no!" she gasped, rapidly turning the steering wheel to avoid having a collision. But the tires spun, and the car skidded off the side of the road toward a telephone pole looming large in her path. As the car hit the pole, she could hear a voice screaming Sean's name and was vaguely surprised to realize that it was hers.

Valerie could feel the mist leaving her brain as the pain came to take its place. She moaned softly as she forced her heavy eyelids open to take in white antiseptic surroundings and a hazy figure in white in front of her.

"Valerie." The low voice persisted in chasing away the cobwebs in her brain.

Her eyes slowly focused, revealing a gray-haired man in his late fifties bending over her. "Dr. Taylor?" she murmured, moving her head slowly, then wincing from the pain shooting through her head. "Wha-what happened?"

"A telephone pole ran in front of your car." His concerned expression changed to a smile of relief. "I'm just glad you decided to wake up from your nap. Now, tell me how many fingers I'm holding up." He showed her his three middle fingers.

She squinted her eyes. "Three," she whispered. "What's wrong with me?"

"You have a concussion and a variety of cuts and bruises," the doctor replied, his hands gentle and sure as he injected something into her arm. "This is for the pain. You just rest now. Your husband is outside wearing a hole in the carpet. I'll send him in after I've spoken to him."

Unbidden, a vision of Felicia in Sean's arms flashed through her mind. "Doctor, where did you find him?" She licked her dry lips.

"At his office, of course." He appeared surprised by her question.

In the small waiting room, Sean was looking morosely out the window and smoking a cigarette. His face was gray under its tan, making him appear older.

"Mr. Hunter?" Dr. Taylor stepped into the room as Sean quickly turned around.

"Is she all right?" he asked hoarsely, crushing his

cigarette into an ashtray overflowing with the remains of numerous others.

"She has a concussion that will give her a bad headache and quite a few bruises," the doctor replied. "I would like to keep her here overnight for observation, just as a precaution. She did take a long time to regain consciousness."

"May I see her?" Sean's voice was anxious.

"As soon as the nurses get her settled." Dr. Taylor motioned for Sean to be seated. "How's young Michael doing? Going on all cylinders, as usual?"

Sean's tense features relaxed. "He never seems to stop." He smiled, lighting another cigarette. "I didn't know kids could have so much energy."

"I've seen him since he was three months old. Valerie's been working hard for him ever since. She deserves a rest, but it's too bad it has to be this way."

At the doctor's words, Sean's hands shook and he was forced to stub out his cigarette.

Dr. Taylor got to his feet. "I'm sure you can go in to see her now. She may be a little drowsy from the medication I gave her to ease the pain." He smiled warmly. "She's a stubborn little minx, but I can't imagine her any other way."

Valerie was slightly drowsy when the door slowly opened to reveal Sean, carrying yellow roses in a vase. He set the vase on the table next to the bed before sitting uneasily in the nearby chair. His dark eyes took in the bruises on her face and shoulders and the large bruise on her forehead. "You've given me a scary time, angel," he said huskily, his voice betraying his emotions. "It's been a long day."

"I'm sorry that I took you away from work," Valerie muttered, her voice thickened from the medication.

Sean's breath hissed, a sure sign of frustration. "You mean more to me than my work does," he stated flatly.

"Is Michael all right?" she asked quickly. "You won't let him get too frightened, will you?"

"I called Sara and asked her to pick him up at school," he replied. "All he knows is that you have to stay in the hospital overnight. No gory details." Sean hesitated before adding, "Sara mentioned that she had offered to take him to school today. I owe you an apology."

"You don't owe me anything," Valerie said dully, turning her face away from him to hide the tears. Why had he been with Felicia? And why couldn't she have the courage to confront him with it?

"Val, please don't turn away from me." His soft voice was pleading as he leaned forward, taking one of her hands in his. "Talk to me. Don't be this way."

"I'd like to go to sleep now," she whispered, fighting the urge to face him, to draw his arms around her for warmth and comfort.

The room was silent save for the soft closing of the door, leaving her alone with her misery. Only then did she allow the tears to fall onto the pillow unchecked until she fell into a drug-induced sleep.

The next morning, Valerie was picking at her breakfast when Dr. Taylor entered the room. "Ah, good, some color in that pale face." He patted her cheek. "Now, if you'll be a good girl and stay in bed for a week to ten days, I'll let you go home. Otherwise, you'll have your vacation here."

"I can't stay in bed for that long," she protested, struggling to sit up.

"Then no discharge," he said firmly.

"But Michael—we've never been apart." She stopped seeing a familiar look of determination on the doctor's face. "I feel fine; I don't see why I need to stay in bed."

"Precautionary." He held her wrist, checking her pulse. "You have a visitor outside. But only for five minutes," he added warningly.

Valerie ran her fingers through her sleep-tousled hair. Her eyes widened as Craig stepped inside after Dr. Taylor left the room.

"Hello, Val." He smiled faintly. "I'm glad to see you aren't badly hurt."

"Thank you, Craig."

He came forward, gripping her hands. "Val, Sean isn't worth it," he persisted. "Come with me. I know you care for me. You have to."

"Craig, I can't." She tried to withdraw her hands.

"I know you care for me. It was obvious at the dance." His blue eyes darkened with desire.

"At the dance?" Valerie was confused by his words.

"On the terrace, when you kissed me," Craig said impatiently.

The horror of that evening came back, causing her to recoil. "Oh, no!" she moaned, remembering the accusations she had thrown at Sean.

"Oh, Val." He lifted her hands to his lips.

She snatched them away, her eyes dark with revulsion. "Please go away, Craig," she pleaded, feeling the nausea rise.

"But Val—"

"My wife asked you to leave, Saunders." A voice of steel invaded the room.

Craig opened his mouth as if to protest, but one look at Sean's cold face caused him to think twice. "I guess you won't be coming back to work, then, will you?" He looked at Valerie's downcast head before he turned and left the room. She didn't look up when a small leather case was deposited on the bed.

"I brought you a change of clothes." Sean's voice was impersonal, as if speaking merely to a friend. "I'll be outside taking care of your discharge."

She didn't look up until he left the room and a nurse entered. "Thought you might need some help getting dressed," she said cheerfully. "You're going to be stiff for a while, so you'll need to take it easy."

Sean had thoughtfully chosen a cotton caftan that zipped in the front and was comfortable against her tender skin. She winced as her stiff muscles refused to respond when she tried to stand up. She was grateful to find a hairbrush and face cleanser also in the case. She felt better as she was wheeled outside. "Hospital rules, dear," the nurse explained to her.

Sean stood by the passenger's door of the large silver car and his hands were gentle as he helped her in. Valerie dourly noticed the nurse's face light up when he smiled his thanks at her before walking around the car to the driver's side.

Valerie rested her head against the back of the seat, closing her eyes. "Dr. Taylor gave me a prescription for some pain pills in case your head begins to bother you," Sean told her as he started the car. "He also told me that you have to stay in bed, and that's where you're going as soon as we get home."

Valerie wanted to protest, but she already felt tired and silently admitted that a bed would feel very good to her. "I want to give you my apology," she said slowly. "I didn't know until today that it was Craig that night at the dance. I just want to say I'm sorry."

"I saw you and Saunders on the terrace that night." Sean's lips twisted wryly. "At the time I thought it was a passionate love scene, but I realized differently later." He inserted a cassette tape into the tape deck, letting the music put an end to any conversation.

By the time they reached the house, Valerie's head was throbbing. As Sean stopped the car in front of the house, Sara came running out. "Oh, you poor dear," she clucked, as Sean opened the passenger's door, lifting a protesting Valerie effortlessly in his arms.

"I can walk," she informed him, feeling self-conscious with her face so close to his, his after-shave drifting into her consciousness.

"Dr. Taylor wants you to stay off your feet as much as possible," he replied, walking into the house. He said over his shoulder, "Sara, could you please bring her something cold to drink?"

"Of course." The housekeeper disappeared toward the kitchen.

Sean carried Valerie to her room, where the bedcovers were turned down invitingly and a light blue nightgown was lying across the covers. He gently set her down on the bed, saying, "Unfortunately, there's an emergency at the office, so I have to go in for an hour or so. I'm sure you'll want to rest for a while. Michael's at preschool today, so I'll pick him up on my way home."

"Thank you, Sean." She smiled faintly, surprised by his unexpected kindness.

His fingers lightly stroked the soft skin near a dark bruise on her chin. "I'd offer to help you undress, but I'm sure you'll only try to convince me that you can do it all yourself," he said drily. "I'll see you this afternoon." He walked toward the bedroom door.

"Sean, how badly is my car wrecked?" she asked, unwilling to see him leave, especially with thoughts of Felicia at the back of her mind.

He hesitated before replying. "It was totaled, Val," he said softly. "There's nothing left."

"The first car I ever owned." She sighed, feeling as if she had lost a dear friend. "I guess I should have had the brakes fixed a long time ago."

"You think it was your brakes?" His tone was curious.

"Yes, I think they may have locked." She shrugged her shoulders as she reached down to slip off her sandals.

A sharply indrawn breath was his only reply before he left the room. Valerie winced as she straightened her arms to unzip the caftan, slipping it off her shoulders. Once the nightgown was over her head, she felt exhausted and lay against the pillows, breathing deeply.

"And that's where you belong," Sara said briskly, entering the room with a tray. "I brought you tea and a snack. Hospital food can take away anyone's appetite."

"I was there for only one night, Sara." Valerie smiled, warming under the older woman's attention.

"One night is long enough." She set the tray on a

small table by the bed. "And I doubt you'll find custard like mine in any hospital. Sean said doctor's orders are for you to stay in bed for about ten days, and I'm to enforce that rule when he isn't here. If you want anything, you give me a call. I'm baking lemon tarts for Michael, but I can hear you. You do have a few things here to occupy your time, though."

Valerie noticed the books on the bedside table, books she had been meaning to read for a long time. "Thank you, Sara."

"Thank Sean. He's the one who got them for you." She walked out of the room. "And be sure to thank him properly," she called back over her shoulder.

Valerie dutifully ate the custard and sipped a cup of hot tea before her eyelids began to droop and she drifted off to sleep. When she awoke, the afternoon sun was setting and a small figure was perched at the foot of her bed.

"Oh, Mommy!" Michael's coloring book fell to the floor as he scrambled across the bed and hugged her tightly around the neck. "Your face is all colored." A sticky finger carefully touched the bruise on her forehead.

"They'll go away," she assured him. "Have you been a good boy?"

"Daddy played dominoes with me, and Sara gave me a bath." His nose wrinkled with distaste.

Valerie's laughter sounded light and carefree as she hugged her son. The sound died in her throat as she looked up to see Sean's lean figure leaning lazily against the doorjamb. He was disturbingly attractive in dark gray slacks and a pale gray silk shirt, unbuttoned halfway to his waist, showing the bronze muscled hardness of his chest.

"I-I'm afraid now that you know how to play dominoes, Michael will never leave you alone," Valerie said breathlessly. "It's his favorite game. He can play it for hours and not tire of it."

"All in a day's work for a father." He shrugged his shoulders, his eyes settling on his son. "Sara said to tell you your dinner is ready. I think you better wash your hands first, though."

"I washed 'em this morning," Michael protested.

"Well, wash them again, just in case."

"Aw," he muttered, climbing down from the bed.

"Michael believes that soap is a boy's worst enemy," Valerie said, feeling self-conscious in the filmy gown that accented her small breasts and smooth skin.

"I did, too, once upon a time." He grinned. "I thought you might prefer eating dinner in the den for a change. I can set up a tray for you next to the easy chair. The television's in there, too, and I have some paperwork to catch up on."

"I don't need to be entertained, Sean, like a small child." She sounded sullen. "I can take care of myself."

"The doctor also said that using the Jacuzzi would help keep your muscles from stiffening up," he went on, ignoring her childish behavior. "I can take you out there after dinner, if you'd like."

"Walking will help just as much," she said stubbornly.

Expelling an angry breath, Sean walked into the room with a panther's lithe grace. He sat on the edge of the bed, his hands lightly gripping her shoulders. "Val, the real reason that you're confined to bed is because of all your bruises, especially those on your legs. For all the doctors know, you could have a blood clot," he said grimly. "Do you understand what I'm trying to say?"

"That if I do, it could . . . shift?" she asked through stiff lips, her face pale from the impact of his words. "That's what you mean, isn't it?"

Sean's hands lightly caressed her shoulders. He dropped a gentle kiss on her forehead before standing up. Walking over to the closet, he rummaged through the interior, pulling out a dark blue robe and throwing it on the bed. "I'll be back in fifteen minutes."

Valerie quickly brushed her tangled hair and slipped on her robe before Sean returned. She felt uneasy as he picked her up and carried her to the main part of the house.

A small table was set up next to a black leather lounging chair in the den. A straight-backed chair sat opposite. The delicious aroma of baked ham teased Valerie's nostrils. After Sean had carefully set her down in the chair, he walked to the other side of the table and sat down. She looked up, surprised. "Aren't you going out tonight?"

"As I told you, I have quite a bit of paperwork to catch up on," he replied smoothly, deftly cutting her ham into small pieces and then picking up his wine-glass. She looked pointedly at her glass of iced tea, then over to his wine. "I should think you'd realize that with all your medication, wine could be a very dangerous beverage for you," he told her logically.

All through the meal, Sean was the pleasant dinner companion Valerie remembered from the early days of their marriage. He spoke about his work and told anecdotes that caused her to laugh, bringing a glow to her pale cheeks. She wasn't hungry, though, and only pushed her food around on her plate. She silently wondered what excuse Sean had given Felicia for not being with her. She knew he had been with her all those other nights, when he wasn't home. Sean was a man with a man's physical appetites, and Felicia was just the kind of woman to satisfy them. Val bent her head, her hair falling forward. She put up her hand and tucked it behind her ear. "It's getting long. I guess it's time for another haircut," she said breathlessly as his eyes fell on her shiny tresses.

"No!" Sean's voice was hoarse. "Don't cut it. Let it grow long again."

Valerie looked at him, searching for some sign. Of what, she wasn't sure, but perhaps something that would tell her that he was softening toward her. Then a picture of Sean and Felicia in front of the store that day flashed before her eyes and she withdrew.

After dinner, Sean excused himself, murmuring about paperwork, and he retired to his study. He left the remote control for the television near Valerie as a pajama-clad Michael bounced into the room carrying one of his storybooks.

Later that evening, after Sara had led Michael off to bed, Valerie fiddled with the remote control, trying to find an interesting program to occupy her time. She wasn't used to any type of inactivity and was so rarely ill that she was fidgety. It wasn't long before the noise of the television wasn't helping the throbbing in her temples and she quickly switched it off. Resting her head back, she closed her eyes, hoping the throbbing would disappear, and soon she fell asleep. She didn't awake until a pair of strong arms scooped her up, holding her close against a warm body.

"My head hurts so much," she whimpered, resting her cheek against the silk-covered chest.

"I know, love." A soft voice sounded in her ear.

Still half-asleep, she was set on her bed and her robe was slipped off by gentle hands. She murmured in protest as a pill was slipped between her teeth and water sloshed against her dry lips. Her head was lowered to the pillow and she soon fell into a deep sleep.

In the middle of the night, Valerie murmured in protest as she found herself standing outside of town wearing only her nightgown. She stood in the middle of the road, feeling bewildered as she looked down the empty highway. Suddenly, a cloud of dust appeared some distance away. A large truck drove down the highway at a high speed and headed straight for her. Afraid, she began to run, looking over her shoulder. The driver's face came into view and she stopped in shock as she saw a grinning skeleton at the wheel. Valerie opened her mouth, screaming Sean's name as the skeleton disappeared from the truck and reappeared standing next to her, taking her arm to lead her away.

"Val, wake up! You're having a nightmare." Sean's voice floated through the heavy mist of her dream, causing her to reach out. His warm arms wrapped around her, cradling her body against his chest. He murmured in her ear, soothing her as she sobbed raggedly. He pushed the damp hair away from her tear-stained face.

"It was horrible!" She gulped air, trying to slow her racing heart.

"It's all right now. I'm here." His hands cupped her face, drawing her back so that he could see it. "The shock of your accident just caught up with you, that's all. You'll be fine in a minute."

"Oh, Sean," Valerie whimpered, clutching him around the waist and laying her cheek against his bare chest where the lapels of his robe parted. A faint light shone over his shoulder and, looking up, she noticed a open door to another room. He followed the direction of her glance.

"My room. That's why I was here so quickly," he explained, putting a hand against her forehead. "You do feel a little warm. Is your head still bothering you?"

She shook her head "no" as Sean gently disentangled himself from her arms. "Think you could go back to sleep?" he asked. "In fact, if you'd like, I'll leave the door open."

Visions of the skeleton made Valerie grab his hands. "Sean, please don't leave me alone," she begged. "I'm so afraid. I can't stay here by myself."

"Val, it wouldn't be a good idea." He hesitated as he looked down at her tear-stained face. "Oh, Val, you know what a mistake this is," he groaned, throwing the bedcovers back and picking her up. Sean carried her into the other room and deposited her on his bed. Sean turned out the light and discarded his robe before climbing into bed beside her. Valerie shivered with fright in the dark room until his arms brought her next to him, laying her head on his shoulder. "Now let's both get some sleep," he muttered, hugging her close.

Sean's body heat lulled her into a warm cocoon and

she was soon able to fall asleep. When her nightmare started to return, her body tensed but his arms tightened, letting her know he was there.

Valerie didn't wake up again until late morning. She pushed her hair away from her face and focused on her surroundings. She sat up slowly, surprised to find herself back in her own bed, although she didn't remember Sean carrying her back. Unless it *all* was a dream?

"Sara." Her voice quavered, then rose in pitch. "Sara!"

When the housekeeper entered the room, Valerie was pale and wide-eyed. "So you finally decided to wake up?" She smiled warmly. "Sean said to let you sleep as long as you wanted."

"Di-did Sean go into his office?" Valerie's voice trembled as she tried to clear her fuzzy brain.

"No. He's out back cleaning the pool. I'll bring you some breakfast now that you're awake. Want me to help you to the bathroom?"

Val shook her head. After Sara left the room, she swung her legs around, setting them down gingerly. She gasped as needlelike pains shot up her legs. Gritting her teeth, she walked slowly to the bathroom and washed her face and brushed her hair, clipping the sides away from her face before hobbling back to the bedroom.

"What the devil!" An angry Sean, clad only in dark brown trunks, stood in the bedroom doorway. "What are you trying to do?"

"I'm trying to make myself look a little more presentable, that's what." Valerie gritted her teeth.

"And hurt yourself more in the process, obviously."

He swung her up into his arms, carrying her back to her bed.

"No!" Her tears fell from pure frustration. "I'm not so sick that I can just lie here not caring what I look like. I haven't had a bath in three days, my hair is filthy, and I feel as if I've been through World War Three!"

"Would you like Sara to run you a bath after you eat breakfast?" Sean asked her. "On second thought, don't answer. I'll just have her do it."

Valerie looked up and glanced at the interconnecting door, now closed. She chewed her bottom lip, uncertain how to phrase her question.

"You had quite a nightmare last night." Sean read her thought. "I brought you in here when I got up; you were sleeping so soundly you didn't even stir." His tone hardened. "After all, I'm sure you wouldn't want Sara to get the wrong idea about us."

"Of course not," Valerie muttered, remembering how content she had felt sleeping in Sean's arms the night before.

"I'll keep that door open from now on in case you need me," Sean commented before leaving the room.

She sat on the bed, hurt by his implied rejection. He made it obvious that she was nothing more than someone who had been very frightened and needed solace. She reached down to the end of the bed, slipping her arms through the sleeves of her robe just as Sara walked in carrying a tray. A fluffy omelet graced the place along with juice and toast. "I want to see all of that gone when I get back," she said with mock severity. "Then we'll get you washed and feeling better."

Valerie was grateful for Sara's help as she carefully stepped into the deep tub full of scented bubbles. "I feel so helpless," she sighed. "I'm not used to having people wait on me."

"Then just relax and enjoy it," Sara suggested, patting Valerie's bare shoulder. "While you're in here I'm going to make your bed up with clean sheets, and I'll also bring you a clean nightgown. But don't try to get out of there by yourself."

Valerie relaxed in the warm water, ruefully examining the dark bruises on her legs. She reached for a small mirror and cried out when she saw the puffy bruises over her forehead and on her cheek. She hadn't bothered with a mirror when she had brushed her hair earlier, so she hadn't seen them before.

"What's wrong?" Sara ran in, holding a pale blue floral pillowcase.

"Oh, Sara, I look terrible!" she moaned as the older woman took the mirror from her hand. "I look as if I've been in a barroom brawl."

The housekeeper's tense features relaxed. "I don't think you need to wory. Sean is just happy to have you in one piece. He was pretty upset when he called me from the hospital. They wouldn't tell him anything, and he was worried that it was more serious than they'd let on."

"You wouldn't know it now," Valerie mumbled to herself.

The days passed slowly for Valerie. She soon finished her books and chafed to be up and about. She was surprised by Sean, who stayed home until mid-morning and generally came back home by late afternoon; he usually shared breakfast with her and was always home in time for dinner. She soon looked forward to his company and their conversations together. She spent her days by the pool, soaking up the sun and turning a deep gold; the bruises gradually faded until she could cover them effectively with makeup.

One afternoon, feeling more restless than ever, Valerie quickly changed into black leotards and tights and pulled on her leather ballet slippers. She walked down the hall to the practice room and closed the door behind her.

A few minutes later, Sean walked into the house, loosening his tie and flexing his shoulder muscles wearily. Michael ran in behind him, happily making noises like a train.

"You change into your play clothes before you do anything else," Sara told him, as she came into the hallway carrying a dust cloth. "Then come out into the kitchen for your cookies and juice. Now scoot."

"Where's Val?" Sean looked around the hallway.

"Don't know." Sara shrugged her shoulders. "I haven't heard a peep out of her since lunch. She might be taking a nap or reading in her room."

"I'll go take a look." He walked away from her. "Be prepared to hear a choo-choo-train story Michael learned today. I've already heard it—twice."

Since the door to Valerie's room was open, Sean glanced in, noticing that it was empty except for some clothes lying on the bed. A faint sound caught his attention and he turned to follow the music that led him to the door of the practice room. Quietly opening the door, he saw her at the barre doing pliés, her face pale from the exertion.

"Val, what are you doing?" he demanded, walking into the room, his face dark with anger.

"It's known as a plié," she replied, counting the beats under her breath before stopping and wiping her forehead with the back of her hand. "I've been idle too long. I need to get my muscles working again."

"It's only been a week," Sean informed her.

"Even after a few days the muscles stiffen up," she protested. "A good workout is the only thing that helps."

"And that's why you look ready to drop!" His dark eyes scanned her paper-white face. "The doctor specifically told you not to have any strenuous exercise."

"Sean, to me this isn't exercise. It was once a part of my life," Valerie said quietly, placing her hand on the barre to balance herself as she slipped off her slippers. "I used to practice six hours a day, and although I'd be exhausted, afterward I'd feel as if I had accomplished something."

"If it hadn't been for Michael, you could have gone on with your career," he said thoughtfully. "Who knows what could have happened? I wouldn't be surprised if there were times when you resented *both* of us for halting those dreams."

"Resent Michael?" Her eyes blazed with sudden anger. "I love Michael more than life itself. Right now, he's all I have." She turned and ran out of the room.

Sighing heavily and feeling angry with himself, Sean walked out of the room.

Fighting angry tears, Valerie ran into her bedroom, slamming the door behind her. She peeled off her leotards, leaving them in a heap on the floor, then walked into the bathroom and turned on the shower.

The warm spray soon relaxed her. Afterward, she wrapped a towel around her wet hair, slipped on a robe and walked over to the dresser where she opened one of the drawers, pulling out a large leather-bound book. She sat on the bed and opened the book to reveal color pictures of a dark-haired baby. Turning the pages, she studied the pictures of a younger Valerie smilingly holding Michael as a small baby. She looked up, startled, as a knock sounded at the door and Sean walked in. He glanced down at the book in her lap before looking up at her face. "I want to apologize for upsetting you," he said ruefully. "I seem to have a knack for it."

"It's just that Michael is very dear to me," she replied in a low voice, close to tears.

Sean leaned down, picking up the large book, and leafing through the pages. He stopped at one of a chubby Michael obviously learning to walk, helped by his mother's hands holding onto his. Valerie was smiling, yet there was a look of haunted sorrow in her eyes.

"Who took the pictures?" he asked finally.

"Shelly or her fiancé, Greg. Shelly said I should have some memories of Michael as a baby. The first picture was taken at the hospital when he was just a few hours old."

Sean turned to the front of the book, studying the color picture of a tiny red-faced infant with his wrinkled face screwed up, as if ready to cry at the camera's intrusion. "Sean Michael Hunter, Jr." He read the name embossed in gold on the cover before handing the book back. "Sara said dinner will be ready in half an hour." He turned to walk to the door.

"Sean, wait!" Valerie jumped up impulsively. "Michael had his picture taken at preschool recently. Would you like one of the large ones?" She walked over to the dresser and picked up a large photograph from the open drawer. The small boy in front of a neutral background wore an open-necked shirt and had a big smile on his face.

"Thank you, Val," he said huskily, looking down at the photograph in his hands. "I appreciate your giving me this."

Valerie stared at the closed door for several minutes after Sean left, realizing that her impulsive action had showed her just how much Sean really cared about Michael.

Throughout dinner, Michael chattered away about his day at preschool and repeated the new story his teacher had told the class. "Miss Karen told Miss Janice that Daddy's really cute and she'd like to be around to pick up the pieces," he said innocently. "What pieces is she talking about? Is something going to break?"

Valerie's fork clattered to her plate. "If you'll excuse me, I'm not hungry," she mumbled, rising to leave the table, but Sean's hand on her arm forced her sit back down in her chair.

"You won't need to wonder about it, son, because there won't ever be any pieces to be picked up," he said silkily, his eyes flashing a warning to Valerie. "So don't think about it anymore."

Her stomach rejected all thought of food. When Sara brought in dessert, Val quickly stood up, picking up plates and serving dishes. "I'll help you with the dishes." She hurriedly escaped to the kitchen. She tied an apron around her waist and began running the hot water, rinsing off the dishes and stacking them in the dishwasher. Sara came with the rest of the plates. She raised her eyebrows slightly but said nothing as she placed the dishes on the countertop next to the sink.

"Michael wants you to go swimming with them in an hour," she said casually. "The exercise will do you good."

"I'd like to start helping around the house since I don't have a job to go back to." Valerie's voice was just as casual as she changed the subject. "This is a large house and there's so much to do."

"I planned on thoroughly cleaning all of the guest rooms," Sara replied without hesitation. "We can start in the morning after the breakfast dishes are done."

The tension left Valerie's body; she turned and smiled at the older woman. "Thank you," she whispered.

Chapter Seven

By the time Michael, tired from his after-dinner swim, was bathed and in his pajamas, Valerie was as exhausted as her son. She tucked him under the covers, closed the door behind her, and walked outside to the patio.

Sean, wearing only his damp swim trunks, was seated on one of the lounge chairs, staring out over the pool. He looked up as she sat on the other chair and leaned back.

"Would you like some wine?" he asked quietly, reaching for the decanter and glasses Sara had set beside his chair.

"Yes, thank you." She accepted the glass of aromatic liquid.

"He go to sleep?" Sean bent his head slightly as he lit

a cigarette, drawing on it deeply and then exhaling the smoke.

"He was asleep by the time I left the room." She sipped her wine.

Valerie was aware of how alone they were and of the quiet house behind them. Sara had left for her own room after bringing the wine out. She smiled wryly to herself, thinking that to an outsider they appeared to be a very happily married couple. Sean had talked to her more during these past days than he had at any other time. In San Francisco they had preferred to make love—to speak with their hands and lips. Her hand trembled at her thoughts as she raised the glass to her lips, gulping the wine.

"That's not water, you know." Sean's low, amused voice reached her ears.

"I'm not a child," she snapped defensively.

"Sometimes I wonder," he muttered, stubbing out his cigarette.

Valerie glanced at the rock-hard figure near her. Four years had not changed the broad chest or lean hips encased in dark navy trunks. He lit another cigarette, the orange flame from his lighter momentarily throwing his rangy features into shadowed relief. She remembered the first time she had seen him by the firelight at the beach. The ache in her body deepened to an undefinable pain.

"I'm going to bed." She set her glass down abruptly and leaped to her feet. She had reached the door when Sean's murmured "good night" reached her ears. As she opened the door she turned slightly, seeing him sitting on the lounger, a brooding expression on his face, as if his thoughts were far away. Once in her room, she quickly showered and then donned a shortie nightgown.

She was sound asleep when something woke her up. She shot up, pushing her hair from her face and looking around the darkened room, seeing only a faint sliver of light where the connecting door was ajar. She got out of bed, walking to the door and swinging it open. Sean was on the bed, propped up by pillows, reading. He looked up with surprise as she stood in the doorway. "I'm sorry. Did the light wake you?"

"No, I—uh—I don't know what woke me up." She shrugged her shoulders.

"Perhaps you had a nightmare," Sean said impersonally, returning to his book. "Do you have any sleeping pills left?"

"They leave me too groggy in the mornings. I don't like to take them."

"Then what do you want *me* to do?" Sean demanded tensely, placing a bookmark between the pages and laying the book on the night table. "Do you want me to tuck you in? To hold your hand until you fall asleep again?"

"I'm sorry I bothered you," she said crossly, turning away.

He swore fiercely under his breath as he got off the bed and stalked over, grabbing her arm and spinning her toward him. "Val," he sighed heavily, "you're not a sick little girl anymore, so this isn't a good idea."

The tip of her tongue appeared, wetting her lips. "Why not?" she asked huskily, raising her eyes to his face.

"You know very well why not." Sean sounded

exasperated as he ran his fingers through his hair. "So just go back to bed."

A perverse notion kept her rooted to the spot. "I can't go back to sleep." Valerie's heart felt as if it would leap out of her body. She reached out to straighten the lapels of his robe. He grabbed her hands.

"You're playing with fire, infant," he growled. "Get out of here—now!"

"But I'm not an infant any longer, Sean," she protested, feeling the power she had over this man and over his emotions. "I have a son to prove it. Your son."

He grabbed her hair, pulling her head back before his lips descended on hers in a punishing kiss. He ruthlessly parted her lips, devouring the sweetness within. Valerie could feel her knees weaken and had to hold onto his lapels for support. His lips travelled down her jawline to her throat and he put one arm under her knees, picking her up to cradle her against his chest. Realizing his intent, Valerie momentarily panicked. "Sean?" she whispered, fear in her voice.

"You've gone too far this time, angel," he said grimly, dropping her on the bed and switching off the light before shedding his robe. "This time you'll have to pay the piper."

When he stretched out beside her, her arms curled around his neck, pulling him to her. Their passion, so long dormant, ignited to a roaring flame. Valerie lost all inhibitions as Sean's mouth and caresses induced a response which she freely gave. She was soon lifted to heights of ecstasy she had never dreamed of as he possessed her. Their hunger for each other diminished, they fell asleep in each other's arms.

* * *

When Valerie awoke, the sun was streaming through the curtains onto the large bed. She stretched, a contented smile on her face. Her smile widened as she remembered Sean's lovemaking the night before and her own whole-hearted response. She sat up and looked around, found her nightgown on the floor, and slipped it over her head. She heard the sound of a shower running and soon shutting off. Sean walked into the bedroom, a toweling robe tied around his waist. He stopped short as he saw her smiling face.

"You're awake," he said unnecessarily. "Sorry if the shower woke you up."

"It didn't disturb me." Her smile disappeared as she noticed his uneasy stance. She wanted him to come over to her, to hold her in his arms and tell her he still loved her. After all, didn't last night prove that? "Sean, I—"

"No, me first, Val; I just want to apologize for last night."

"Apologize?"

"Yes, for taking advantage of you." His halting words chilled her heart. "After all, you hadn't had any wine for quite awhile, and it had obviously affected you. I should have insisted you go back to your own bed. There's no excuse for what I did. I can only say I'm sorry."

"Then all I was to you was an outlet for your manly urges?" Her lips twisted bitterly, causing him to wince as if with pain.

"Nothing that sordid," Sean said bleakly, refusing to meet her eyes.

Valerie scrambled out of the king-size bed, pushing aside the beige sheets. "Then I guess I should also apologize for thinking that your intentions were honorable. I'll be sure to stay out of your way from now on." Her head held high, she left the room without looking back.

Sean stepped forward, his hand outstretched as if to stop her, but he seemed to change his mind and checked himself.

Valerie closed the door behind her, deliberately flipping the lock. She showered away Sean's touch and then slowly dressed in jeans and a cotton T-shirt. She skirted the dining room, where she knew Sean would be breakfasting, instead using the door leading to the kitchen.

Valerie was grateful for Sara that day. She was able to forget her hurts when they decided to rearrange the living room. They pushed the furniture to the center of the room before deciding where to place the various pieces. She was pleased with the final results. The morning passed quickly until Sara called a halt for lunch. "I'll fix us something while you make up the beds." She walked toward the kitchen.

Valerie quickly made Michael's bed, then hers, before slowly entering Sean's room. She had only been there late at night, and this time she was able to examine it more fully. The king-size platform bed dominated the room; night tables of light-colored teak were attached to the headboard. A large chest of drawers was placed against one wall, while a large nine drawer dresser stood opposite. It was obvious that the furniture was meant for a man and wife, and it appeared to be fairly new. She threw back the dark brown bedspread and quickly stripped off the sheets. She got clean sheets with tan, gold, and brown stripes from the linen closet and made up the bed, smoothing the bedspread over the sheets and pillows.

Then she entered the bathroom, still scented with his aftershave, and put out clean fluffy towels of a camel shade bordered with dark brown. She noticed that the cap was off the tube of toothpaste and smiled faintly, remembering the many times she had scolded him for doing that. Her smile disappeared in a look of pain. "Oh, Sean, why do you do this to me?" she whispered, squeezing her eyes shut to stop the tears. "Do you hate me that much?"

Late that afternoon, Valerie was peeling potatoes at the sink when Michael ran into the kitchen with Sean close behind. He raised an eyebrow at her and she bristled, aware that she wore no makeup, had on old, dirty clothes, and that her hair was untidy.

"Oh, Mommy, you look funny." Michael wrinkled his nose at her.

"That's because Sara and I moved furniture today." She planted a kiss on the top of his head.

"Should you be doing that?" Sean frowned with concern as he loosened the dark blue-and-gold-striped tie at his throat.

"For goodness sakes, I'm fine and healthy, not pregnant!" Valerie snapped irritably, then could have bitten her tongue when she saw the dark look on his face. The horror of it all was that for all she knew, she *could* be pregnant; and they both were aware of it.

"No, you're not, are you?" he said quietly, before striding out of the room.

Her only concession to dinner was to wash her hands

and face and spray on a light perfume. She quickly brushed her hair, clipping it back from her face, then looked down at her jeans but defiantly decided to keep them on.

Valerie felt uneasy sitting at the table with Sean, but it appeared that he was equally uneasy around her. Her busy day had sharpened her appetite and she soon cleaned her plate.

"You keep that up and we'll have some meat on those bones yet," Sara said approvingly. "I'll do the dishes tonight. You just sit down and relax for a while."

"Play dominoes with me," Michael demanded. "Please."

"One game," she said firmly, "and one only. Then it will be time for your bath and bed."

"Aw, Mom." He screwed up his face.

"A bath," Sean said quietly in a voice meant to be obeyed.

"When I—"

"I know—when you grow up you're not going to take baths," Valerie and Sean said in unison, then looked at each other in surprise.

Later that night, she could see a sliver of light under the connecting door, evidence of Sean's wakefulness. She lay on her side, watching the faint light until her eyelids dropped with sleep.

Valerie was exhausted and when she finally awoke the bright sunlight announced that it was mid-morning.

"Oh, no!" she moaned, looking at her clock. She threw back the covers and jumped out of bed. A quick search of the house showed that it was empty; it was Sara's day off and she had planned to run some errands of her own. A note was propped against the coffeepot in the kitchen.

Didn't want to disturb you so we made our own breakfast.

S.

Valerie poured herself a cup of coffee while debating how to spend her day. The shimmering pool looked inviting, but she knew she'd feel guilty later on for not keeping up with the housework. She spent the morning cleaning her bedroom, then putting the houseplants outside for a thorough soaking with the hose.

Later that afternoon, she collapsed in a chair, gratefully drinking a tall glass of iced tea. She looked up in surprise as the door chimes pealed softly. "Who can that be?" she wondered aloud, getting up and walking toward the front door. She opened the door to reveal a tall woman in her early thirties dressed in tight jeans and an equally tight gauzy cotton shirt. She stood on the doorstep, hands in her pockets, and long, sun-streaked, dark blonde hair tied back with a silk scarf. Large sunglasses were perched on top of her head as she smiled warmly at Valerie, seeming to remind her of someone, but the resemblance eluded her.

"Hi. Is Sean around?" she asked brightly.

"No, he's at his office," Valerie said cautiously. Was this another one of his girl friends? A new one, perhaps? After all, she hadn't seen Felicia for a while.

"You must be Valerie." The woman's tone was friendly. "Sean's written me about you."

"He has?" Now she felt completely confused.

"I'm Janine, his sister," she explained. "Didn't he ever tell you about me? Or am I the skeleton tucked away in the closet?" She gave an amused chuckle, her brown eyes dancing with mischief.

"Well, come on in," Val offered, relief evident in her eyes.

After carrying Janine's suitcases to her old room, the two women walked toward the kitchen. "How about something cold to drink?" Valerie asked.

"I'd love that. The air conditioning in my car hasn't been working all that well for the past hundred miles."

"Sean said you paint." Val opened the refrigerator door, bringing out a frosty pitcher.

"I guess you can call it that." Janine shrugged her shoulders.

"I saw some of your work at your house and it was beautiful," Valerie said sincerely, filling two glasses.

"Thank you. I need all the critical praise I can get." Janine gratefully accepted her glass. "And I understand you dance."

"Not seriously anymore." Val shook her head.

"But you *were* going to dance school when you and Sean were married."

"Michael changed all of my plans," Val replied softly.

"Michael?" Janine looked puzzled.

"My son." She looked up, surprised. "Didn't Sean let you know?"

Janine's face broke into a glowing smile, a feminine version of Sean's. "No, he didn't, that rat," she gurgled happily. "You mean I'm an aunt? Well, when was he born? Can I see him?"

"Michael will soon be entering the 'ferocious fours.' He's at preschool right now. Sean picks him up on his way home from the office," Valerie explained.

"Then I take it that darling big brother learned about

his son only recently, because I saw him a year and a half ago and he didn't even mention a son—and it's not something he'd keep a secret." Janine leaned forward in her chair, continuing bluntly: "Why did you leave Sean?"

"It's a long story," Valerie mumbled, keeping her eyes glued to the table.

"I know I shouldn't have asked, but the artist in me likes to probe below the surface. Look, Valerie, I hit thirty a few months ago, and the reason I'm not married is because there's only one man like my brother. Sean and I may fight like cats and dogs, even though we only see each other every few years, but I love that guy because he's all male. You won't find one better. That's why I'm so glad to see that the two of you are back together. Sean needs a very special woman, and I already feel that you're that woman."

Valerie squirmed uneasily in her chair, all too aware of the real reasons behind their reconciliation. "I guess I should start dinner."

"Oh, can I help?" Janine asked eagerly. "I may not be a gourmet cook, but I haven't poisoned anyone yet." The two women talked companionably as they worked in the kitchen.

"Chicken in wine sauce is my specialty." Janine delicately licked her fingertips. "But I can whip up a mean trifle, too." Valerie opened a cabinet and turned as the back door opened and Michael ran in. He stopped short, staring curiously at Janine.

"Oh, Val, he certainly is Sean's son," she breathed, squatting down on her heels. "Hello, Michael, I'm your Aunt Janine."

"Aunt Ja——." He stumbled over the name.

"Try Aunt Jay; it's much easier." She smiled. "I'm so pleased to meet you."

Sean walked in with his suit coat flung over one shoulder, his eyes narrowed as he saw his sister. "Well, Jay, to what do we owe the occasion?" he asked coolly.

"I came for a nice family visit, brother, dear." She was oblivious to his tones. "Don't worry, darling, I'll be a good girl. I promise. Cross my heart and hope to die." She smiled, full of impish charm. "After all, I am your baby sister."

"Little did my parents know," Sean growled, but his eyes were warm as they rested on her. "They might not have taken that vacation."

"Now you know why I see him only every few years." Janine turned to Valerie. "Well, I think I'll go change for dinner and wash off the rest of this road dust."

"I guess I'll go change, too," Valerie muttered, not wanting to be alone with Sean. "Come on, Michael."

She took her time choosing her outfit, but finally settled on a long, multi-colored cotton skirt and a white cotton peasant blouse that showed her figure to advantage.

She stopped by Michael's room and called to him. "Why don't you come help me set the table?"

"Boys don't set tables," Michael said scornfully.

"Then you can help *me.*" Sean's voice sounded behind her. "We'll both set the table for your mom."

"But Dad, we don't have to do it. That's for mommies to do."

"Michael, your mom's done two jobs for quite a while." Sean's eyes met Valerie's over their son's head.

"And now it's our turn to help her out. That way she won't get her pretty clothes dirty."

Valerie was surprised that he noticed her outfit, especially when she compared it to Janine's. Janine wore deep purple cotton knit trousers and a simple light lavender top with spaghetti straps. Her hair was twisted on top of her head in a simple knot and large silver hoop earrings completed the ensemble.

"You still haven't told us the reason for honoring us with your presence," Sean said drily as he poured the wine into three glasses.

"None for me," Valerie murmured, flushing as she remembered the last time she had drunk wine. The glint in Sean's eyes showed that he read her thoughts.

"I told you, a friendly family visit to meet my new sister-in-law and, it seems, my nephew. Now, why don't you tell me about this new firm of yours? I'm still surprised that you left the army. And tell me all the local gossip."

Valerie felt left out as Sean and Janine discussed mutual friends. The discussion continued through dinner until Janine suddenly changed the subject. "Sean, I'd like to see this sister-in-law of mine in some of the newer fashions. Val has great style, a good figure, and is *very* attractive; she just needs to show it off more."

"I don't need any clothes," Val protested, not wanting Sean to pay for anything of hers.

"As long as you promise to leave something for the other women," he said drily, "go ahead and shop. Just give me the bills."

"No problem there." Janine smiled sweetly at him.

"I can't possibly wear all of these clothes," Valerie said, surveying all her boxes with dismay as they walked out of the store the next day.

"That's why I told Sean to take my car and we'd take his." Janine grinned mischievously. "His has much more room, *and* I was almost out of gas. Bet he loved that."

"But we spent too much money," Val said ruefully. "He's going to be furious. He's just starting a new business, and he can't afford all of this."

Janine stopped dead in her tracks, shocked, then burst out laughing. "Oh, Val, you really don't know, do you?" She giggled, shaking her head in amusement.

"Know what?" Val felt bewildered.

"Sean has no money problems at all," Janine said gently. "Our grandfather was a real estate speculator and, to put it bluntly, died filthy rich. Our father increased the investments and everything was left in trust to us until we each turned twenty-five."

"But Sean was in the army," Valerie persisted, feeling confusion set it.

"Brother Sean is a graduate of West Point. Didn't he ever tell you?" Janine opened the trunk of the car, piling packages inside. "He stayed in the service only because he enjoyed it; it's only been recently that he's wanted to settle down in one place. I use my money to pay for my trips and the expenses for my house; Sean uses his for his business. He's been friends with this other engineer for a long time, and they just decided to start their own firm." Janine slammed the trunk lid shut. "Now, I suggest we run by the office of our object of discussion and coerce him into taking us to lunch. Then we can finish our shopping this afternoon."

"I still think Sean is going to kill me," Valerie said slowly, starting up the engine of the large car. She knew where Sean's office was located but had never been there. It was in a modern business complex in the middle of town. A discreet gold plaque hung on the door: HUNTER & EASTMAN ENGINEERING, INC.

A well dressed young woman in her early twenties sat at the reception desk. She greeted them with a warm smile.

"Would you please tell Mr. Hunter that his wife and sister are here to see him?" Janine informed her.

The receptionist pressed a button on the intercom, speaking softly into it. "Mr. Hunter's secretary, will be out in a moment." She smiled at them.

Valerie wandered around the reception area, nervously studying the paintings on the walls.

"Mrs. Hunter?" A voice sounded from behind.

Valerie turned to face a tall, dark-haired woman in her late twenties. A simple skirt and print silk shirt of a deep rose shade accented her coloring. "I'm Barbara, Mr. Hunter's secretary." She smiled. "Mr. Hunter will be in a meeting for a few more moments, but he would like you and his sister to wait for him in his office. Would you come this way, please?"

She led them down a paneled hallway to an outer office. A desk, file cabinets, and typewriter showed that it was obviously her own. She opened the door to an inner office, gesturing toward a tweed sofa along one wall and two easy chairs.

"Would either of you like coffee?" she asked, receiving negative shakes of the head from both women. "Mr. Hunter will be here soon." She closed the door behind her.

"I guess Sean doesn't believe in hiring little old ladies," Janine commented drily.

"She has the right image for the office," Valerie replied, feeling unhappy after seeing Sean's secretary. They must be more than employer-employee. She walked across the office toward a large walnut desk with a black leather chair behind it, curious to see the view; but her attention was arrested by a gold double picture frame sitting on a corner of the desk. She picked up the frame, studying the two photographs: the one of Michael that she had given him, and one of Val herself, taken on the day she and Sean were married. Looking at the picture, she was surprised to see how young she looked, so carefree and happy.

She turned, hastily putting the frame down, when the door opened and Sean walked in. His eyes seemed to light up when he saw her. "This is a surprise." He nodded toward Janine. "You two run out of money?"

"We thought you would enjoy taking two beautiful women out to lunch," Janine said brightly.

Sean's eyes met Valerie's, the dancing lights in them telling her that he knew whose idea it really was. "Nothing I'd enjoy more," he said smoothly. "I hope you realize we'll have to take my car instead of your two-seater—if there's any room left, that is."

"Enough," Janine said airily.

Sean stopped at his secretary's desk long enough to tell her that he'd be gone for lunch. "Those specs are ready to be delivered to Thayer's. I should be back around one-thirty."

As they walked down the hallway, Valerie was very aware of Sean, walking close behind her. "Barbara is very happily married to a county sheriff and has three daughters," he murmured in her ear, "and don't try to act the dim-witted female. I'm sure you wondered about her."

She held her head higher, ignoring the fact that, once again, he had read her mind. Sean's low chuckle told her that he knew exactly what she was thinking.

"What about that good barbecue place?" Janine suggested.

Sean looked questioningly at Valerie, who nodded in agreement.

"I love the barbecued beef here," Janine told Valerie later as they were seated in a booth. "That and their corn on the cob and their apple pie."

"Then she complains she's getting fat," Sean said. "Well, how much did you spend this morning?"

Valerie blushed as she drew the receipts out of her purse and slowly handed them to him. He barely glanced at them and stuffed them in his shirt pocket before turning to her. "I meant what I said, Val—get what you need," he said softly.

"If you two will excuse me, I'm going to freshen up." Janine rose hastily.

"I told Janine that I shouldn't spend so much money," Valerie said in a low voice, "and she told me about your grandfather. I never knew; I feel like such a fool."

Sean covered her hand with his, sighing. "I was going to tell you, but I didn't know how. You seemed to enjoy working out budgets at the time, and I didn't have the heart to tell you that you didn't have to worry about it. But then there was no need to."

"Oh, Sean, we're so different. Don't you see that it will never work out?"

Sean's eyes narrowed at her thoughts. "Perhaps because you won't give yourself any credit for your own talents," he said roughly. "You're still acting like a child, not a woman."

"I wish I had never come out here," she declared hotly. "If you'd ever told me anything about yourself, I would have known that you lived here and you can bet I would have ended up as far away as possible!"

"I would have found you, Val, and I wouldn't think of trying it now if I were you." Uncannily, he had read her thoughts. "The consequences would not be nice."

She felt miserable throughout the rest of the meal. Sean ignored her, talking exclusively to Janine, who looked surprised but said nothing. After lunch, they dropped him off at his office and drove back to the shops.

By mid-afternoon Valerie called a halt, saying she couldn't walk another step. "We spent more this afternoon than we did this morning," she sighed wearily. "All I want to do is go home and have something cold to drink." She stopped short, realizing that this was the first time she had referred to Sean's house as home. That's the way it seemed to her now: home, something she hadn't had since her parents died.

They picked Michael up at the preschool and he shrieked with delight at the new baseball, mitt and bat they had gotten for him. He begged them to play with him as soon as they arrived home.

"Never sure who's the child," Sara mumbled, setting a pitcher of iced tea, two empty glasses and a third filled with juice on a table outside. Michael happily swung his bat at the careful pitches Valerie threw to him. Janine stood behind him as catcher.

"Look at our star player here." A deep voice brought three pairs of eyes around. Sean lounged lazily in one of the chairs, a cigarette between his fingers.

"I hit the ball, Daddy!" Michael said excitedly, dropping his bat and running toward the man. "Mom threw it and I hit it past her."

"Keep it up and you could get signed up by the major leagues." He gazed fondly at his son. Then his eyes traveled upward to Valerie, the warmth gone. She brushed the hair away from her sweaty face, all too aware of her grubby shorts and T-shirt. With all of her new clothes hanging in the closet, she had chosen to wear the oldest things she had. Sean drew on his cigarette, coolly looking her over. "Part of your new wardrobe?"

"Of course not," she replied crossly.

Just then Sara called out to them, "You've got one hour till dinner. I suggest you get cleaned up before you show up at the table."

"I think she means us." Janine grinned at Valerie. She turned to Sean. "What about you, big brother?"

"I'll finish my beer out here first." He drew slowly on his cigarette, not looking at either of them.

As they entered the house, Valerie looked back to see Sean crush his cigarette in the ashtray with a savage gesture. She yearned to go back and sit at his feet and lay her head in his lap as she used to do. But she knew he would only reject her with a scornful gesture, and she couldn't stand any more rejection, especially not from him.

Valerie stood under the shower, letting the water cool her heated emotions. After washing her hair, she wrapped it in a towel and surveyed the large assortment of makeup she had bought that day. With a dancing glint in her eyes, she stood before the mirror, artfully adding touches of eyeshadow, liner and dark mascara to her eyes, and a dusting of a rose blusher to her cheekbones. Then she finished drying her hair, pinning it in a loose knot on top of her head with curled tendrils on the sides and nape.

She enjoyed going through her new clothes and finally chose a white cotton sleeveless top banded in black. It was almost backless and the low, rounded neckline showed off her golden tan, and the bottom ended above the waistband of her black pants, showing several inches of tanned midriff. Black sandals, gold earrings, and a delicate gold chain completed the provacative outfit. After painting her nails a deep rose shade, she let them dry and liberally sprayed herself with perfume before leaving the room.

Janine was already in the den sharing a drink with Sean when Valerie entered. Her eyes lit up impishly while Sean's narrowed fractionally as he noticed the generous portions of bare skin. "I just knew that was made for you. You definitely have the slim waist for it. What do you think, Sean?" The smile she flashed her brother was totally innocent.

"Aren't you afraid of showing more than you intended?" His words were forced through his teeth as he quickly poured himself another Scotch and swallowed it just as quickly.

"Perhaps Val would like a drink," Janine prompted silkily.

Sean silently mixed Valerie's gin-and-tonic, and she was careful that their fingers didn't touch his as she accepted the glass. His eyes lingered on the wide expanse of bare midriff before traveling upward over the low neckline, resting for a moment on her rounded breasts, before stopping at her pinned-up hair and gold hoop earrings.

"I came up with a great idea for this evening." Janine was more bubbly than usual. "And I was just discussing it with Sean. There's going to be an informal get-together at the country club tonight. So why not go? It should be lots of fun."

"We can't leave Michael," Val protested, unwilling to continue this farce in public. She was so tired of hiding her true feelings from Sean.

"Sara has already volunteered to keep an eye on him." Janine airily dismissed her qualms. "We'll have a ball, won't we, Sean?"

"Why not?" He shrugged his shoulders, his eyes sending Valerie a mocking challenge. "It should be interesting."

Throughout dinner, Valerie was aware of Sean's veiled glances at her low neckline. She shifted uncomfortably in her chair, trying unobtrusively to pull it higher. An amused smile tugged at the corners of his mouth, causing her to flush with embarrassment. Slow burning anger soon replaced her discomfort. He *knew* he was making her uncomfortable, and he was enjoying it! She gritted her teeth as she endeavored to eat her stuffed pork chop and rice pilaf. Conversation between Janine and Sean floated over her downcast head.

"So you got rid of your Jaguar a year ago," he commented, refilling his wineglass. "It was a nice car.

I'm sure Val remembers that car," he added wickedly, bringing a flush to her face.

"I just like smaller cars." Janine sipped her wine. "The Jensen Healy is fine for my needs."

"Faster, too," he said drily. "The way you drive, that car won't be around by the end of the year." He abruptly turned to Valerie. "I'm sure you're going to want to change before we leave for the club."

Stung by his high-handed attitude, she retorted hotly, "I'm just fine."

"Suit yourself." He turned back to Janine, resuming their conversation.

Janine changed before they left for the club. She wore flame-colored silk pants with a matching strapless top and a loose, long-sleeved print blouse that tied at her waist. Her honey-colored hair was left loose to her shoulders. "You should be flattered to escort two such beautiful women, brother dear." She smiled sweetly at Sean.

"Aren't you afraid of catching—cold?" He addressed his remarks to Valerie.

"Not at all." She lifted her chin.

The short ride seemed an eternity to Valerie. Her nostrils pricked at the subtle scent of Sean's aftershave; she longed to reach out and touch his arm or stroke his cheek as she had been used to do. But she knew better by now. She clenched her hands together as she painfully recalled the feel of those strong hands so knowingly caressing her bare skin. She suddenly realized that she was being spoken to. "What? I'm sorry, I didn't hear you," she stammered, looking up.

"Wake up, Val." Janine laughed, snapping her fingers in front of Val's face.

Sean's mouth quirked, as if he had read her erotic thoughts. "While you've been dreaming, we've arrived at the club."

They waited in the doorway for Sean to park the car. Valerie's eyes turned toward a familiar sports car in the parking lot. Craig was here! She hadn't seen him since he had visited her in the hospital. Oddly, she didn't feel angry toward him anymore; his fierce devotion had kept her ego up when she had needed it most.

Valerie's heart contracted violently as she watched Sean stride across the well lit parking lot. His shoulders were broad in the cream silk shirt tucked into the dark navy slacks, belted low on his hips. The lights shining on his tanned features reminded her again of the first time she had met him. The moonlight played over the carved features and she remembered how he had both fascinated and frightened her at the same time.

As they entered the building, Sean's arm rested possessively across her shoulders. Just an act for his friends, she thought bitterly to herself. Well, two could play at this game. "Darling, could you possibly get me a drink?" she asked brightly.

"I thought you might have had enough at dinner." His eyes narrowed.

"I'm just dying of thirst, though," Valerie pouted. "Please, Sean."

"Go on, Sean, get us our drinks while we mingle," Janine urged. "I see people I haven't seen in ages. I'll introduce Val to anyone she doesn't know. We'll be just fine."

"That's what I'm afraid of," he muttered under his breath, walking away.

"Celia!" Janine enthusiastically greeted a woman of about her own age. "It's so good to see you!"

"Jay, I didn't know you were back." Sherry-colored eyes looked over Valerie.

"This is my sister-in-law, Valerie." Janine turned toward her. "Val, Celia Howard and I went to school together."

"So you're Michael's mother." Celia smiled warmly. "My Keith attends the same preschool. I usually see Sean picking Michael up at the school—at least I have for the past month or so," she commented. "I understand you had a car accident."

"A telephone pole decided to get in my way," Val said ruefully.

"The epitome of a woman driver." A deep voice from behind startled the three women. Sean handed Valerie and Janine a glass of wine each before draping his arm over Valerie's shoulders, an action both possessive and deliberate.

"Hello, Celia," he greeted her genially. "How is your tribe doing?"

"As wild as the Indians they should be." She laughed, then explained to Valerie: "We have three boys, and the fourth will probably be one, too. I've given up on having a girl."

Valerie felt a pang of envy toward this woman and her family; it was obvious that her husband, although he was not visibly in evidence, loved her.

"Where's Rick?" Sean asked, looking around.

"The billiard room—where else? He doesn't believe in dancing, as I've known for many years. I can't expect him to change now," she said ruefully.

"Then I'm sure you won't mind if I dance with *my* wife," he said suddenly, reaching for Valerie's glass and setting it down on a nearby table.

"You don't have to dance with me," she said stiffly, as they walked toward the dance floor. "I'm sure it isn't expected."

"It isn't, but perhaps I want to," he replied enigmatically, drawing her into his arms. The touch of his hand against her bare back was electric, sending shock waves throughout her body. She tried to lean away from him, but a firm pressure brought her against his chest and held her there.

"You're not being fair," she hissed fiercely.

"Angel, I never promised to be fair." His fingers tantalized her bare skin in a sensuous stroking motion.

"Sean, stop it!" Her low voice trembled, and Valerie felt close to furious tears by the time the dance ended.

"I'm sure you'll be happier on your own." Sean released her and walked toward the other side of the room. Her anger grew as she saw him greet Felicia Everst warmly as the woman's hand came to rest intimately on his arm.

Valerie picked up her wineglass and, looking around the room, soon saw the man she was looking for. Draining the glass, she fixed a smile on her face and caught his eye. Craig looked surprised at her inviting smile and cautiously approached her.

"Hello, Val." His voice was wary as he appreciatively eyed her slender figure.

"How are you, Craig?" Her low voice was almost a purr.

"To be honest, surprised that you'd talk to me after all that's happened." His eyes finally rested on the soft curves of her breasts where they showed above the low neckline.

"I was upset then, because of the accident," Valerie murmured, feeling satisfied as Sean glanced their way and his eyes narrowed to angry slits. "But that's behind us now. You *are* going to dance with me, aren't you?" She held out her arms invitingly.

Before Craig could reply, a steel vise clamped around Valerie's wrist. "Excuse us, but we have a family matter to attend to." Sean's voice was cold and controlled. Keeping his bruising grip on her wrist, he almost dragged her out of the club to the parking lot.

"What do you think you're doing!" she demanded, the alcohol she had consumed giving her extra courage. "Let go of me!"

"Not until we reach the car." He spit out the words. "You sure couldn't wait to get back to Saunders, could you? Another minute and you would have found yourself in bed with him."

"I hate you!" she cried out suddenly as his fingers tapped her cheek in a light slap.

Sean grabbed her hair, pulling loose the pins and letting it fall around her face in loose waves. "Don't you ever do that again," he growled, his temper barely in control as his nostrils flared whitely.

Recklessly, Valerie tried to twist away from him, only to feel her neck snap back and have her mouth bruised under his punishing kiss. Just as she began seeing dancing lights and thought she'd surely faint, she was suddenly released.

"Go to —!" she finally managed to choke out, only wanting to hurt him as much as he had hurt her.

"You put me there four years ago, angel," he interrupted roughly, "and now you'll pay for it—every day of your life."

"The agreement was only for six months," she whispered, tight-lipped, feeling the defiance drain out of her body.

"Except that I may change my mind." He pushed her toward the car, none too gently. "Get in before I decide to teach you another lesson."

The ride home was silent and tense. Valerie edged as far away in the seat from Sean as she could.

"What about Janine?" she finally asked.

"I'll go back and get her," he replied crisply, not looking at her.

"And Felicia." Valerie mouthed the words silently, unwilling to incur his wrath once more.

At the house, Sean stayed long enough to see her inside before leaving again. The nightlight was on in the hallway, guiding her to her room. When she flipped the switch on, she was surprised to see a small figure curled up on her bed. "Michael." She shook him gently.

The small boy awoke and threw his arms around her neck. "I wanna sleep with you, Mommy," he mumbled sleepily. "Please, can I?"

"Of course, darling." She planted a light kiss on his forehead.

As Valerie lay awake in the quiet house, she was glad for the small body curled up next to her. She felt comforted in a way she hadn't felt in a long time. Putting an arm around Michael, she soon closed her eyes and fell asleep.

Chapter Eight

"Val! Val!" A pounding on her bedroom door brought her slowly awake. She sat up in bed, trying to focus her sleep-drugged eyes as Janine burst into the room. "What's going on?" She yawned, pushing her hair away from her face.

Janine looked suddenly relieved as she saw a waking Michael next to Valerie. "Sean, he's in here with Val," she called over her shoulder. A moment later, Sean appeared in the doorway, his tense features beginning to relax.

"What's going on?" Valerie asked again groggily, still trying to shake off the effects of sleep.

"We couldn't find Michael. It appears he's been in here all the time," Sean stated flatly, running a weary hand through his hair.

"He had a nightmare and asked to stay with me," Valerie explained.

"How the devil were we supposed to know that?" His voice rose angrily.

"Mommy, why is Daddy mad at us?" Michael whimpered, curling up closer to her.

"Come on, love, let's get you dressed," Janine suggested, picking up the small boy in her arms. "Then we'll get some breakfast."

"There was no need to upset Michael," Valerie said heatedly, climbing out of bed uncaring of the flimsy nightgown that barely reached her thighs. "He's only a little boy. He doesn't understand this constant war between us, and I won't have him hurt by it!"

Sean's eyes flicked coldly over her bare legs. "I suggest you put some clothes on." His lip curled in disgust as he spun on his heel and walked away.

Angered beyond control, Valerie unclenched her hands and, looking for the first available object, picked up a book from the night table and flung it at one of the walls. Her blind aim sent it against the mirror, shattering the glass. She stomped angrily into the bathroom, slamming the door behind her.

A brisk shower eventually cooled Valerie's anger. She dressed in bright green terry-cloth jogging shorts and a green-and-white-striped terry tanktop. Walking back into the bedroom, she found Janine seated on the bed with several pieces of paper in her hand.

"Seven years' bad luck, you know." She gestured toward the broken mirror.

"If so, then I only have three more to go." Valerie smiled bitterly.

"Val, please sit down." Janine's voice became serious. "I'd like to say something to you."

Curiosity won out as she sat on the bed next to her sister-in-law.

"It wouldn't take anyone with an ounce of brains to see that things aren't well between you and Sean. Separate bedrooms speak for themselves, and I happen to know my brother well enough to know that it couldn't have been his idea. He just isn't the type of man to put up with that kind of thing."

"The only reason I'm even here is because he wants Michael," Valerie said bleakly. Sensing the other woman's sincere compassion, she blurted out the entire story, including the traumatic night years before. Janine remained silent throughout. "So you see, I'm only here on a pass, so to speak," she concluded bitterly. "He feels nothing for me but disgust. The sooner I'm gone, the happier he'll be."

"If he doesn't care for you, he has a funny way of showing it," Janine chuckled softly. "I've never seen him so angry as he was last night when he saw you with Craig Saunders. In fact, he was livid. And as to the disgust . . ." She held up the papers in her hand. "This is part of a letter he wrote to me a long time ago. I kept it because of the contents, and I'd like you to hear part of it." She bent her head slightly, looking at the large sprawling handwriting:

Dear Jay,

Well, I know this will be hard for you to believe, but I was married a week ago. My only excuse for not letting you know sooner is that it's been too difficult to tear myself away from my beautiful wife. So you'll have to forgive me for not inviting you to the wedding, but I was afraid that if I waited too long I'd lose her. I wasn't going to take any chances.

To begin with, her name is Valerie. She's studying ballet at a school here in San Francisco. She's not very tall, slender as a reed, with long dark hair and eyes the color of jade. From the first time I met her, I knew I had to make her mine.

Some people will probably call me a fool because she's only twenty: innocence combined with seductiveness; youth with maturity. I don't tire of her company because she is a constantly changing individual.

I guess you can tell that big brother fell—and fell hard—for an enchantress who has a smile to outdo the morning sun. I can't wait for you to meet her because I know the two of you will get along so well. You can't help but love my green-eyed angel.

Sean

Janine looked up to see slow tears trickling down Valerie's cheeks. She pushed the papers into Val's hands. "I want you to keep this," she urged. "Something like that doesn't die, no matter what. Sean is a proud man; you've hurt his pride badly and he won't let anyone know it. But be patient; he'll come around." Tactfully, she left the room.

Valerie stared at the letter, unable to believe Sean had written such beautiful words about her. She carefully folded the sheets of paper and put them away in her night table drawer. After washing the tear stains from her face, she brushed her hair, leaving it loose, and headed for the dining room.

Sean was already there, with a subdued Michael seated next to him, glumly eating scrambled eggs. Janine was seated across from Michael, acting as if nothing had happened.

"Your omelet will be ready in a moment." Sara stuck her head through the swinging door.

"I'm afraid I'm not very hungry, Sara," Valerie muttered, refusing to look at Sean as she seated herself. "Juice and coffee will be fine."

"I am fixing you an omelet and you will eat every bite," Sara replied tartly. "And no arguments."

"Everybody's mad today," Michael sighed heavily.

Sean turned toward his son, smiling fondly at the downcast face. "Are you finished with your breakfast?"

Michael nodded his head as he finished his glass of orange juice. Sean leaned over, whispering conspiratorially in Michael's ear. The small boy's face lit up like a Christmas tree. "Can I go now?" he asked eagerly, climbing down from his chair.

"As long as you stay there until I call you." Sean tousled his hair.

Although curious about the exchange between father and son, Valerie's pride wouldn't allow her to ask. When her omelet was placed before her, full of creamy cheese and bacon bits, Sara eyed Valerie's set face. "Eat," she ordered, as if Valerie were a small child. "You're still too skinny for my taste."

"I always have been," she said crossly, noting the faintly amused look on Sean's face.

"Nothing more homey than the family all together for breakfast in the mornings." Janine grinned impishly, receiving only a dark look from her brother. "Just like the soap operas on T.V."

Valerie ate little, instead pushing her food around on her plate.

"If you've finished playing with your food, I'd like to see you outside," Sean said coolly.

She shrugged her shoulders, then rose to her feet to follow him out of the room. At the front door, Sean waited until Valerie caught up with him. "Val, about what I said this morning," he began hesitantly, holding out his hand.

"Message received and noted, Mr. Hunter," she said quietly, raising her eyes to meet his. "I'll take great care never to disgust you again."

His hand dropped to his side and his eyes glittered coldly at her words. Sean opened the door and walked outside, with Valerie following. Her eyes widened as they took in a large green station wagon parked in front of the house. She turned to face a grim Sean. "But—?" She felt thoroughly confused.

"Your own car was totaled and you need transportation," he explained offhandedly.

"It's so big." Valerie walked slowly up to the car, tentatively touching the gleaming surface with her fingertips.

"Not so big when it's loaded with kids and pets!" Janine laughed behind them.

"One small boy doesn't constitute—" she began, but was cut off by her son's excited shrieks.

"Mommy!" Michael ran from the back of the house holding a furry bundle almost as large as he was.

Valerie turned accusing eyes toward Sean. "You did this," she said angrily, gesturing toward the car, then toward the wiggling bundle in Michael's arms.

"Oh, Val, he's darling," Janine protested, taking the squirming puppy from Michael's arms. "What are you going to name him, love?"

"Muffin," he announced proudly. "And he's all mine."

"Sean, he can't have a puppy," Valerie appealed to the tall man, "especially one that looks as if it'll grow up to be the size of a small horse."

"Labrador retrievers don't become small horses," he said blandly. "Besides, having the responsibility of caring for a dog will be good for him."

Valerie looked around wildly but saw that she was outnumbered. Michael was sitting on the ground, cooing to his new friend. She turned back to the car, knowing a new car was something she had never dreamed of owning.

"Next time you decide to wrap yourself around a telephone pole, I want you to have more car for protection." Sean's low voice was close to her ear. "Plus it saves you from having to borrow my car. So the least you can do is smile sweetly and say, 'thank you, Sean.'"

"Thank you, Sean," she mimicked his words.

He held out two keys, pressing them into her hand. "One is for the ignition, and the other is for the front and back doors," he explained before turning and walking away.

Janine approached her, hands stuck in pockets. "Let's go inside. I'd like to talk to you.

"Val, I've decided to go back home tomorrow." She

sat down on Val's bed and began without preamble. "It's time for me to dig out my paints again. I'll probably stay home for six months to a year. What I'm trying to say is that I want you to feel free to come and stay with me if you need some breathing time."

"It's not that bad, Jay," she said evasively.

"My brother is a darn fool!" Janine exploded, rising to her feet and hugging Valerie. "It would serve him right if you walked out on him today."

"I did that once—four years ago," Val said bleakly. "As a result, he missed out on the first four years of his son's life. He'll never forgive me for that."

Janine shook her head in frustration. "You just remember that if you need a shoulder to cry on, you know where I am. I can tell that you want to be left alone, so I'm going out to the pool. I'll see you at dinner."

After Janine left the room, Valerie lay on the bed, her thoughts tumbling together so rapidly that she began to feel a pounding in her temples. "Oh, Sean, why couldn't I just have said I'd go to Australia with you in the first place?" she whispered to herself, feeling an ache in her throat. Exhaustion soon took over and she fell asleep, curled up in a tight ball.

A few hours later, when she awoke, she discovered Sean standing over her, an inscrutable expression on his face. "Sara asked me to tell you that dinner will be ready soon." His tones were clipped as he straightened. "Janine is taking one of her day-long bubble baths."

"I'm sorry you had to be bothered, then." Valerie's voice held a trace of bitterness as she sat up.

Sean's eyes rested on the tanned cleavage visible between the parted lapels of her robe. Seeing the direction of his gaze, she flushed, hurriedly wrapping the robe close around her.

"I found this not too long ago and thought you might be interested." He reached into his shirt pocket and tossed a small jeweler's box into her lap. Then, silently, he turned and left the room.

Valerie looked down, a soft "Oh!" escaping her lips as she held up two delicate jade earrings, a perfect match for the pendant he had given her so long ago, and the pendant itself, which she had never expected to see again. "Oh, Sean, what are you trying to tell me?" she sighed heavily. "Does this mean the beginning? Or the end?"

Standing up, she walked over to her closet and searched through her new clothes. After careful deliberation, she chose a simple strapless dress of clinging jersey in a subdued green and wore both the new earrings and the pendant. She used electric rollers on her hair, brushing it into soft curves, and a little more eye makeup than usual. The final effect was understated, yet seductive.

"I knew I was right about that dress," Janine said triumphantly when Valerie later entered the den.

"Mommy looks sexy," Michael announced to his father, looking up from his storybook.

"Sexy? Where did you learn that word?" Sean demanded, scowling at Valerie.

"Like father, like son?" Janine hinted. "I understand one of Michael's friends thinks he's sexy. He's already becoming a hit with the girls."

"He has plenty of time," Sean muttered into his glass of Scotch.

"Think what it would be like if you had had a daughter," Janine pointed out with malicious delight.

"I'd lock her up until she turned thirty." His hooded gaze landed on Valerie. "The way women go around half-dressed causes nothing but trouble. Aren't you afraid you'll lose something?" He stared pointedly at the elasticized neckline.

"The elastic is snug enough." She shrugged her shoulders. "If you don't mind, I *would* like a drink."

Still scowling, Sean mixed her drink and handed her the glass, still staring at her bare shoulders. "I thought you bought new clothes." he said sarcastically.

"I did," she replied, looking up with innocent eyes. "Don't you like this?"

"Too much," he muttered under his breath.

Sean ate very little during dinner, although he frequently helped himself to the wine. As soon as dinner was over and Sara volunteered to take Michael off for a bedtime story, he rose, ignoring Val, and turned to Janine.

"I have a lot of work to catch up on in my study, so I'll see you in the morning before I leave."

She smilingly blew her brother a kiss. "I knew you wouldn't waste the opportunity to say good-bye," she replied lightly.

He abruptly turned and they soon heard the slam of his study door.

"It's a good thing I'm leaving, because I think you and Sean need to be by yourselves." Janine yawned. "I'm not worried, though, because I really believe you two can work things out." She twisted the gold chain at her neck around her finger. "Both of you are just going to have to give in a little, that's all."

"Sean's not the type to give in," Valerie sighed, "even a little."

"Then forget your pride," Janine advised. "It will be worth it in the end. I've seen the change in Sean over the past four years; he's not the man I used to know . . . or the man who wrote me that letter." She rose to her feet. "Well, I guess I should start my packing. I'd like to get a halfway early start."

Valerie found the house empty after Janine's departure. Her parting words lingered in her mind: "Think about what I said last night," Janine whispered to her as they hugged each other good-bye. "Sean's one man in a million."

Sean had taken Michael outside, the puppy happily following them.

Eager to be alone with her thoughts, Valerie wandered into the den, putting some classical records on the stereo. Curled up on the couch, she lost herself in the music and her thoughts of Sean.

With Janine gone, tension had returned to their lives. Sean was usually home in the evenings, or, if he went out, didn't stay out as long as before. Valerie, eager to have something to occupy her time, helped Sara with the housework and drove Michael to and from preschool, loving the feel and ease of her new car. It wasn't long before she had settled herself into a new routine, looking to all the world like a happy housewife and mother.

One morning during breakfast, feeling at odds with herself, she idly pushed around the scrambled eggs on her plate while Sean talked with Michael. "Since the fair is in town, I thought we'd take Michael toward the end of the week," he said, turning to her and lazily sipping his coffee. "We could spend the day there."

"I wanna go! I wanna go!" Michael demanded loudly.

"Sean, he's too young to go anywhere for the day," Valerie protested, puzzled by his invitation and knowing she couldn't spend a day with him without losing the peace of mind she had worked so hard to obtain. "And you said yourself, the office has been very busy lately." And then there's Felicia; I'm sure she's back in the picture by now, she thought cattily to herself.

"They can do without me for a day. And I'm sure Michael will do all right." He rose from the table. "We'll plan on going Thursday, then. We can get an early start."

Valerie was up early Thursday and dressed casually in jeans and a yellow T-shirt. Then she went into Michael's room to help him get dressed. She bent to tie the shoelaces of his sneakers and then straightened up.

"You go out to Sara for your breakfast and I'll be there in a minute," she told him. "And you eat everything on your plate. I don't want to hear that you're hungry an hour from now."

He grinned cheekily at her before running from the room. Valerie went back to her own room long enough to brush her hair and clip it back from her face.

Sean was already at the table, eating his breakfast, when she appeared. He was also dressed in jeans and a T-shirt, his dark hair gleaming damply from his shower.

"Can I please take Muffin to the fair?" Michael begged. "He'll be good, too. I know he will."

"Sorry, pal, but no dogs," Sean told him. "He'll be happier staying home and waiting for you."

Sara came into the room and set a plate of pancakes in front of Valerie. "I want those gone when I come back. You're still too thin for my taste."

Valerie looked at the plate in dismay. "I've never eaten this much for breakfast in my life," she protested.

"If you did, you wouldn't be so skinny," Sara said crisply, before leaving the room.

The corners of Sean's mouth twitched in amusement.

"It's not funny!" she flared up. "I can't possibly eat all of this."

"Eat what you can," he told her.

"No, Mommy, you said I always have to finish everything on my plate, so you should, too," Michael spoke up.

"Get out of that one," Sean murmured, silently laughing.

Valerie sighed heavily as she spread butter on the fluffy pancakes.

During the drive to the fair, Michael bounced up and down in his seat, demanding to know how long it would be before they would arrive at their destination.

"If you don't settle down we'll end up in a wreck; otherwise, we'll be there in a few minutes." Sean pointed off to their right. "We may even find time to walk around the midway and find a merry-go-round."

Michael sat back in his seat, his eyes shining at the prospect. Inside the fairgrounds, he skipped happily between his parents, one hand held by each. His green eyes grew larger as he saw the rows of stables with the heads of the various horses hanging over the stall doors. "Oh, look! There's a spotted horse!" He jumped up and down.

"He's called a pinto," Sean explained. Then he cautioned, "Don't run too close to any of them."

"Can I have a horse of my own, Daddy?" He turned

to look up at Sean. "Can I? I'm getting bigger now. I'm almost four."

"We'll let you add a few more inches on top and then we'll see about a pony for you," he promised.

Suddenly unhappy, Val thought to herself: I don't even need to be here. Sean can decide everything; maybe Michael doesn't need me any more than Sean does. Tears sprang to her eyes at the thought.

They soon left the stables behind, wandering through the various exposition halls, even observing exhibits of farm machinery. When Michael's short legs began to drag, Sean picked him up and reached over, grasping Valerie's hand. His touch burned her skin, but she felt suddenly warm and content to have him so close beside her. When they went back outside, she squinted against the midday glare.

"Now to find a merry-go-round," Sean announced, setting Michael down. "Come on, pal, I'm sure you can walk on your own for a while." He turned to Valerie. "Would you like to stop for a cold drink first? It might help you cool off."

Surprised that he was concerned for her well-being, she could only nod her head wordlessly. An expression she couldn't identify passed across his bronze face as he gazed into her eyes, but it disappeared just as quickly as it had appeared.

"Let's go, then," he said crisply.

Valerie looked around the noisy midway, teeming with games of skill and chance and carnival rides. Handing her lemonade to Sean, she went on the large, colorful merry-go-round with Michael, who sat happily on a large wooden horse.

"Will my horse be as big as this one?" he asked her.

"No, love, quite a bit smaller." She smiled at him.

After lunch at one of the snack bars, Michael's head began to droop with weariness.

"I'm surprised he lasted this long," Valerie said softly, brushing his hair away from his damp face. "It would probably be best if we took him home for a nap."

"Right." Sean adjusted Michael so that the small boy's head rested against his shoulder. He held out his hand to Val with a strange gleam in his eyes. Flashing a warm smile reminiscent of years before, she grasped it as they walked out of the midway area. Several minutes later, Valerie looked around in bewilderment.

"Sean, we're going the wrong way," she protested, gesturing toward her left. "The parking lot is over that way; I'm sure of it."

"One more stop to make." He led her toward an exhibit hall they hadn't gone into earlier.

"But Sean, he's so tired," she told him. "He's half-asleep now."

Inside, Sean walked through the crowds, sure of his destination. Valerie noticed jealously that even the older women glanced at him with admiring eyes. She was surprised to see Sara standing off to one side with a smug smile on her face.

"Sara!" exclaimed Valerie. Then it dawned on her. "Did you enter something?"

"My jam. Won second prize, too," the housekeeper told her proudly, then turned her eyes to the drowsy Michael. "Looks like this young man has had a busy day."

"You said you were going home around three. Would you mind taking him with you?" Sean asked her.

Sara's reply was to hold her arms out for the little boy.

"But I thought we were going home," Valerie said, looking puzzled.

"No. Just Michael. We have the rest of the day ahead of us," he told her. "So let's enjoy it."

"It isn't fair to leave him with Sara," Valerie protested as Sean grabbed her hand and practically dragged her out of the hall.

Outside, he stopped abruptly and faced her, his eyes blazing gold with anger. "Look, he'll be fine with Sara. She'll spoil him and he adores her," he stated flatly. "So, do you want to go to the fair with me, or back home?"

She hesitated briefly, knowing this might be the last time she'd have him all to herself. "I want to go with you," she said softly, raising her eyes to meet his.

His taut features relaxed into a smile. "Then let's not waste any more time," he replied, just as softly.

They spent the balance of the day watching the horse races and the rodeo. As the day faded into evening, they drifted through a midway ablaze with bright lights and carnival music. All the strain had left Valerie's face and she appeared as carefree and happy as a teen-ager. She glowed under Sean's attention as he walked with his arm draped casually over her shoulders. "How about some dinner?" he asked her.

"I have to admit, I *am* pretty hungry."

"Then I better feed you." Sean eyed her slight figure. "Sara's right, you've been much too thin since your accident." His arm tensed against her.

"Now I know enough to look out for telephone

poles." She tried to pass it off lightly, although her mind still registered the horror of that day.

"No, I should have kept an eye on your car since it wasn't in the best of condition," Sean said tightly.

Valerie's heart constricted at the grim expression on his face. "Sean, please," she pleaded, then lightened her voice. "After all, you promised me a beautiful day."

"If possible, I'll do even better than that," he murmured, receiving a puzzled look from her as they walked back to the parking lot.

Not much later, her happy expression disappeared as she saw Felicia approach them, accompanied by a man in his early fifties.

"Well, hello." Felicia greeted them airily, her eyes on Sean. "John, I'd like you to meet some neighbors and close friends of mine, Sean and Valerie Hunter. And this is John Bennett; he's looking into purchasing some land in the area."

The two men shook hands, and the other man nodded smilingly at Valerie.

"Sean is a civil engineer and he might know of some good prospects for you," Felicia told John. "He's a very helpful man to have around." She smiled slyly at him.

Valerie could feel her happiness seeping away as she watched Felicia glance intimately at Sean, although he appeared oblivious as he talked to John about land in the area. He glanced down at Val's stony face, surprised by the sudden change, and soon politely terminated the conversation.

"We must get together very soon." Felicia smiled archly at Sean, touching his arm with her long red-tinted fingernails.

"Well, Val and I haven't had a lot of free time together, so we may hibernate for a while," he replied silkily, disengaging his arm. Felicia's eyes narrowed dangerously.

"Well, I'm sure things will change." Her voice sounded harsh.

"For the better." Sean nodded toward the other man. "Nice to meet you." He took Valerie's arm. "We have to get going. We're late for a dinner engagement."

"Then have dinner with us," Felicia suggested rapidly.

"No. We have previous plans," Sean said smoothly. "Good-bye."

"You didn't have to refuse on my account," Valerie said sullenly as they walked toward the car. "I would have been a good girl and not said anything to embarrass you."

"If I had wanted to go, I would have accepted no matter what tricks you would have tried to pull," he said grimly. "But I didn't care to have dinner with them, although I don't know why I'm even bothering to explain it to you. I'd much prefer for us to dine alone, but if you don't care for the idea, I'll just take you home."

"No, that's fine with me," she said softly, feeling the happiness bubble up inside again.

"Then let's eat because I'm starving," Sean growled, grabbing her hand.

Sean chose a small restaurant that specialized in seafood.

Valerie was reminded of the first time they had been together when he had taken her to Fisherman's Wharf in San Francisco. She now realized how young and naïve she had been then, and how in awe of this worldly man. As she glanced around the dimly lit room, she suddenly remembered that the six months would be over soon. Should she stay with Sean, as a figurehead wife, or should she give up, leave her son to Felicia and Sean and go away? She knew she'd have to go away, because she couldn't bear to live in the same town as Sean and Michael and never see them. She swallowed the lump in her throat, feeling the tears well up. Bending her head over her plate, she concentrated on her delicious meal of deep-fried prawns; she didn't realize that Sean had noticed her trembling hands and slightly quivering lips.

"Val, are you all right?" His voice evinced his concern. He reached across the table, covering her hand with his.

"I'm fine," she hastily replied, pride forbidding her to tell him of her fears and the deep love she still felt for him. Valerie picked up her wineglass, hoping that the alcohol would steady her nerves.

"What would you say about getting Michael a pony for his birthday?" he asked her. "I know someone who's selling one, a good gentle one, not too frisky. Of course, I'd tell him he could only ride it in the corral when I'm with him."

"Whatever you think best," she replied in a low voice.

"Val, I'd like your opinion," Sean persisted. "What do you think about it?"

Valerie knew she couldn't stay at the table any longer. Mumbling an inane excuse, she fled the dining room and ran out to the parking lot. She had barely reached the car, tears streaming down her face, when she was grabbed by the shoulders and roughly turned around.

"*Now* what on earth is wrong?" he angrily demanded, shaking her by the shoulders until her head rang and the tears flowed freely. "Oh, Val," Sean groaned, pulling her to him, "what am I going to do with you?"

"You don't have to worry; I'll go away quietly," she sobbed against his shoulder. "I won't make a fuss."

"Go away? Why?" His face was grim and taut. "Why would you want to go away?"

"Be-because the six months are almost up." Valerie's words were slurred from her tears. "You said—"

Sean swore quietly, making her flinch. "In the car," he ordered, unlocking the passenger's door. "We obviously need to get a few things straightened out, and this isn't exactly the place to do it."

Valerie sat huddled in the seat, sniffing noisily. After Sean settled himself behind the wheel, he took out a handkerchief and turned toward her, tenderly mopping her damp face before starting the car. She stared out the window as the powerful car ate up the miles, and all too soon they were home.

Sean mixed two drinks, handing one to Valerie. "Drink this." He pushed the glass into her hand and sat on the leather couch next to her, giving her time to compose herself.

Feeling a little nauseous from the combination of alcohol and tension, Valerie set her glass down on a small table and started to rise. "Thank you for the drink, but I think I better go to bed," she said faintly.

"Oh, no you don't," Sean warned, grabbing her wrist

and pulling her back down to the couch. "You have some explaining to do."

"About what?" she asked evasively, refusing to meet his eyes.

"Your sudden change of personality—that's what. This morning you were all smiles and ready to go along with any of my suggestions. Then suddenly you look as if you lost your best friend. Now I want to know what's wrong—and I want to know now. And it better be the truth."

"I just have a headache, that's all," Valerie whispered. "Please, I'd just like to be alone. Good night." She rose again, disappointed that he didn't even try to stop her.

"Was it because Felicia wanted us to join them for dinner?" Sean's question halted her retreat. "Or because of my relationship with her?"

Valerie bit her trembling lip as she spun around. "I can't be upset over her being your mistress, can I?" Her voice was pained. "All I want is for Michael to be well cared for when I leave."

"What do you mean, 'leave'?" he demanded, getting to his feet.

Choking back a sob, Valerie turned and ran down the dark hallway, heading for the safety of her room. She gasped as her arms were grabbed and she was spun around against a rock-hard chest.

"Why do you want to leave?" he growled in her ear.

"Y-you said I could stay only six months," she sniffed audibly, "un-unless I was willing to be a figurehead wife so-so I could stay with Michael or else I would have to give him up." Valerie was beyond caring about her pride. "Please don't take Michael away from me," she begged, pressing her palms against his chest. "He's all I have."

"You never meant to contact me about him; what makes you think you're fit to take care of him?" Sean asked cruelly.

"You and Felicia can have other sons. Please, Sean, don't take him away. I don't want to lose anyone else I love," she sobbed.

Sean's icy features softened as he studied her tear-stained face; he framed her cheeks with his palms. "In some ways, Val, you're still a child," he said gently. "Who would ever guess that you're the mother of a four-year-old child and can be a passionate lover? I'm beginning to think that some of those times I made love to you I should have given you a good spanking, instead. And why should I let Felicia have my sons when I have a perfectly good wife already?"

Valerie looked up in disbelief. "But she's your mistress—and you want to marry her," she choked out the words.

"Correction—*she* wants to marry *me*. I had no intentions of marrying her when I dated her years ago, and I only saw her recently to make you jealous," Sean said wryly. "You're the only woman I've ever wanted at my side for all time. And in my bed," he finished huskily.

"Oh, Sean," she breathed, unable to believe her ears, "I love you so much."

Groaning deeply, he pulled her against him, kissing her hungrily, making up for all the time they had lost. His mouth moved sensually over hers, healing her hurts as he drew her closer to him. The spark ignited a roaring flame between them, leaving them wanting more of each other.

"It's a good thing we're married, because I'm not letting you sleep alone tonight—if I let you sleep at all," Sean muttered thickly against her lips. "I can't let you go now, Val. I can never let you go."

An incoherent murmur was her reply as she tightened her arms around his neck, pressing herself close to his body. He bent slightly and slipped an arm under her legs, picking her up and holding her against his chest. She burrowed her face against his neck, pressing her lips against his skin. He headed for the end of the hallway, pushing his bedroom door open and then kicking it shut after them. They were soon enclosed in their own world of passion, rediscovering each other and their love.

Sometime during the middle of the night, Valerie awoke feeling cold and burrowed closer to the burning warmth beside her. Sean's strong arms clasped her against his bare chest, keeping her head in the crook of his shoulder. She turned her face, pressing her lips against slightly salty skin, feeling the steady pulse under her mouth. Fingertips cupped her chin, tipping it upward for his kiss. Sensing her response, his kiss deepened as he shifted his weight, pressing her backward among the bedclothes. Valerie's eyes shone with desire as she linked her arms around his neck, pulling him toward her as they let their passions mount to a high plateau before they fell into a deep sleep once again.

When she awoke again it was just past dawn. She stretched lazily, feeling more content than she had felt in a long time. Smiling to herself, she propped her head on one elbow as she lay on her side, gazing lovingly at the husband she had rediscovered last night. Valerie knew now that their love for each other had not died over the years but had merely slumbered to awaken in passion. She reached out and traced the rugged contours of his face with a fingernail, glad to see that the tension was gone from his face as he slept.

"Don't start something you can't finish." His deep voice was lightly teasing, though his eyes were still closed.

"I should think you'd prefer to rest," she teased. "As Janine said, you're not getting any younger."

Sean reached up and pulled her down to him, nuzzling her neck. "I probably should get even with you for that crack," he growled.

"Oh, Sean, is everything going to be all right now?" she sighed, remembering his words from hours before.

"Don't worry, angel, everything's going to be fine," he whispered to her as he wrapped his arms around her.

Later, he cupped her face in his hands, looking tenderly at her. "I've made you a promise that won't be broken," he told her. "We've been at each other's throats far too long. You've been on the defensive with me ever since you got here, and all I knew was that I had to break through that shell you built up around you."

"But that was because I thought you wanted to marry Felicia," she said sadly. "That hurt the most."

"Well, I'll tell you again—I have no intention of marrying Felicia when I already have a wife who I love very much, although it seemed for a while that she was happier with someone else," he added grimly.

"I should have known it wasn't you on the terrace

that night, that you would never do such a disgusting thing." Valerie felt ashamed for blaming him.

"You were so mad at me that you wouldn't have seen the truth if it had hit you." Sean leaned back against the pillows, pulling her head to his shoulder. "I could have throttled you for not letting me know about Michael. I wanted to punish you in any way I could. But I also knew I had to have you close to me. I started staying away from the house, working instead at the office, because I was afraid of carrying you off to bed and having you hate me even more. Then you had that accident and gave me a real scare. And seeing Craig in your hospital room had me seeing red—I was afraid I had lost the battle until that night when you asked me to stay with you. Then I thought maybe I was being given a second chance. But you were still recovering from your accident; you gave me a lot of lecherous thoughts that night, wench." He grinned wickedly, seeing her flush.

"I was afraid you'd refuse to stay." She idly traced random patterns on his bare chest with her fingernail.

"Stop it," he said thickly. "I want to get a few things straightened out first—especially, why you left me four years ago, leaving me only that note."

Valerie's thick lashes lowered, covering the painful memories written in her eyes. "B-because you frightened me that night." Her voice trembled. "After you left I realized I didn't want to be without you; my dancing was nothing compared to my love for you. Bu-but then you came home later and—" Her voice broke.

Sean's arms tightened convulsively around her. "Oh, Val, angel," he groaned, burying his face in her hair.

"I've been through hell since then. I was afraid to fall in love with you because I was so afraid of losing you. You were so young and innocent, I couldn't believe that you could love me back. I didn't want to lose you, Val—I couldn't. That first time I kissed you I felt as if you had become a part of me."

"Oh, Sean." Valerie's eyes shimmered with tears at his halting words.

"When you talked about staying behind in San Francisco for that part in that dance, I didn't know what to do." Sean's voice reflected the pain he had felt then. "I was afraid you were tired of married life and of me, that you wanted out and you figured it would be an easy way to separate us. All I could do was lash out at you. Being drunk was no excuse for what I did to you, but its the only one I had. I was so angry because I was so afraid. For four years I told myself that I was over you, that you didn't matter to me anymore. But I was lying to myself, angel. I knew you'd be at that party; Shelly told me. I thought I could be so strong, that I could see you and not care, that I could make you miserable and enjoy it. But when I saw you standing there with Craig, I felt as if I had been punched in the gut. Half of me wanted to punish you for running away, and the other half of me wanted to go down on my knees and beg for your forgiveness. I knew I had to have you back, but I didn't know how. And then I found out about Michael and I knew how I could do it, but now I feel so guilty. Can you ever forgive me for the things I said? I'd never take Michael from you, angel; you must know that."

"Oh, Sean, we've wasted so much time," Val murmured.

"Then we'll have to start making up for all that lost time," Sean whispered sensuously as his lips traveled over her face.

"I should check on Michael," she said teasingly.

"If Michael needs anything, Sara can take care of him." He rolled over, trapping her beneath his body. "I think it's time we discussed a brother or sister for him."

"Why discuss it when can handle all the technicalities ourselves?" Valerie murmured, her green eyes glowing with love. She was exactly where she wanted to be and she wasn't going to leave—ever.

READERS' COMMENTS ON SILHOUETTE ROMANCES:

"Every one was written with the utmost care. The story of each captures one's interest early in the plot and holds it all through until the end."

—P.B.,* Summersville, West Virginia

"Silhouette Books are so refreshing that they take you into different worlds. . . . They bring love, happiness and romance into my life. I hope Silhouette goes on forever."

—B.K., Mauldin, South Carolina

"What I really enjoy about your books is they happen in different parts of the U.S.A. and various parts of the world. . . ."—P.M., Tulia, Texas

"I was happy to see another romance-type book available on the market—Silhouette—and look forward to reading them all."

—E.N., Washington, D.C.

"The Silhouette Romances are done exceptionally well. They are so descriptive . . ."

—F.A., Golden, Colorado

* names available on request